Old Moon C

Volume V

Published by Old Moon Quarterly.

Cover art by Derek Moore (https://www.derekmooreart.com/)

Contents

Introduction

Dear Reader,

Kull contemplates his doom upon a shadowed throne. He fears the ephemeral nature of his own consciousness. He touches a world unseen, and wonders if he himself is no less a shadow.

But then he strikes a man down and roars, "by this axe, I rule!"

Such is the dichotomy of Kull: philosopher and barbarian, king and warrior, certain killer and dubious thinker. Robert E. Howard, the modern progenitor of our beloved sword-and-sorcery genre, finished only a handful of Kull stories in his lifetime; among them, the first sword-and-sorcery story of the modern era, "The Shadow Kingdom."

But Kull is, in many ways, a strange pick for the first sword-and-sorcery hero: a thoughtful, contemplative man who ponders the winding complexities of that ancient kingdom he finds himself ruling, yet for all his contemplations, he proves himself a fearless, peerless warrior time and time again. Nevertheless, there is a curious hesitancy to him that many of Howard's later characters lacked. Sometimes, Kull concerns himself with destroying the corrupt and complicated laws and customs governing the peoples over which he rules. At other times, he contemplates his own reality and finds himself bedeviled by shifting meanings he cannot quite grasp. He can, at times, more resemble Elric and other later heroes than he does his fellow red-handed barbarians. He breaks the taboos of his people, and is cast out by them. He adopts a foreign, "decadent" empire as his own, becoming its troubled king. He throws off the clannish prejudices of his life as an Atlantean, becoming battle-brothers with Brule Spear-Slayer, a Pict.

Kull's stories were popular when they were released: "The Mirrors of Tuzun Thune," perhaps Howard's most purposefully psychological story, was a favorite of *Weird Tales* readers. Even so, Howard abandoned Kull. He thought the character too invested in his "psychologicalism," and feared the character was an inauthentic pretension. Only three Kull stories ended up published in Howard's lifetime; the fourth finished one, "By This Axe, I Rule!" was revised into the first of Howard's eighteen Conan the Cimmerian tales, "The Phoenix on the Sword." Conan was evidently a character with whom Howard found himself more comfortable. Conan is not quite the simpleton later pop culture would make him, but he was undeniably less introspective than his Atlantean antecedent.

In many ways, modern sword-and-sorcery—this includes the current revival—takes its cues from Conan rather than from Kull. One can, perhaps, understand the impetus behind this trend: Conan is a devil-may-care, swing-first and damn-the-consequences type of fellow. There is a vitality to him that bleeds off the page in his best outings, an aspirational quality to his indomitable nature. At no point does one fear for Conan in Howard's stories: he *will* win, it's just a question of how. Kull is not so tidy a hero. His doubts plague him. His thoughts wrack him. His fate is left uncertain in "The Mirrors of Tuzun Thune," the questions raised by the text unresolved by its end. Ambiguity has its hooks in Kull in a way that Conan, perhaps, does not achieve (or, rather, does not suffer).

Yet, Conan's imitators are legion. Kull's imitators, if they exist, are less fruitful in their multiplication. It is somewhat trite to speak of discrete "traditions" within sword-and-sorcery: the genre is, and ever has been, one situated on the literary borderland. It's been a site for some profound mixing and blurring of genre lines, even from its very origins (witness the cosmic horror in Conan's greatest outing, "The Tower of the Elephant"), and art ever defies the urge to codify and categorize.

But if we allow ourselves the guilty thrill of succumbing to the categorizing, traditionalizing urge for a moment, might we speak of two threads within sword-and-sorcery: the Conan and the Kull? Certainly, the Conan thread is the larger and the brighter. We often see fewer glimpses of the interiority in these stories, and a greater emphasis on indomitable will and bloody action. Triumph is achieved in these stories—a bloody, desolate triumph, perhaps, but a triumph nevertheless. The Kull thread is—barely—the longer of the pair, and perhaps a bit darker than its brother. We see ambiguity emphasized in these stories, and with it, a greater insight into the interior lives of our various swordsmen and sorcerers. Tragedy scars these stories: we might place Karl Edward Wagner's Kane within the Kull tradition, whose immortality isolates him from his own humanity. Perhaps Elric as well bears the Kullish brand: lord over a fallen people, Elric struggles against the weight of tradition, and questions the nature of his reality more than once (and, of course, dies by the end of his story, slain by his own runesword). Triumphs occur, but they are often of a more qualified nature than those in the Conan tradition; victories purchased that might end up worse than defeat, when all concludes.

At *Old Moon Quarterly*, we love both sorts of stories. And, of course, these categories are themselves somewhat haphazard, even spurious. But we admit: we sometimes wish we saw more stories of the Kull variety. Stories that embrace textual ambiguity and character interiority even as they cleave skulls into red ruin.

To that end, we have a few Kullish stories in this issue. We begin with one, in fact, in Jonathan Olfert's "Together Under the Wing," a tale of stone-age conflict between a guilt-marked mammoth and the giant who slew said mammoth's mother. We conclude with something of one as well, in Joseph Andre Thomas's medieval-horror tinged story, "The Headsman's Melancholy." But in between those Kullish bookends, we have some pure Conanite thrill: Charles Gramlich's "Skulls of Ghosts," which details the bloody exploits of Krieg, the black-eyed wanderer and axeman, and David K. Henrickson's "Well Met at the Gates of Hell," where a character rather like Conan at his most mercenary meets some former comrades and reckons his debts to them.

Alongside these stories, we have some material that (of course) defies the easy classifications we advanced above. K.H. Vaughn's "Champions Against the Maggot King" darkly subverts some epic fantasy tropes and, in the process, delivers us an elegiac story of sword-and-sorcery in a dying world. Amelia Gorman's spectacular "The Origin of Boghounds" combines cosmic horror and a Vancian flare for language and worldbuilding into a delightful and unique story. And, of course, we have our first (but not our last!)

forays into the world of verse. Joe Koch's "The King's Two Bodies" is a melancholic rumination worthy of Kull himself, and Zachary Bos's "A Warning Agaynste Woldes" wields archaic English to grand, and atmospheric, effect.

As ever, we hope you enjoy the prose and poetry collected within this issue as much as we enjoyed curating it.

Kindest regards,

The Editors at Old Moon

Together Under the Wing

By Jonathan Olfert

On the day the Giant King ate his greatest rival, her son came home with blood on his tusk-blades from the war she'd begged him not to fight.

The matriarch Grass-Whisper had lived in a grove in the hills, now stomped flat by vast human-like footprints. Her carved tusks lay in cracked-off chunks; they and the blood were all that remained—that, and the huge flint used to skin her before eating. A flint five times the size of the quartz blades bound to his tusks.

As Grass-Whisper's son took in the tragedy and the horror of the scene, a small and secret part of him felt eager for a battle that wouldn't wrack him with regret. Recognizing that inspired further guilt, because if—when—he killed the Giant King, his purpose should be pure, unselfish vengeance.

His mother had called him Sweet-Onion as a boy. For ten far-ranging winters, peoples of many kinds had known him—feared him—as Walks-like-a-Rockslide.

One shuffling, weary step at a time, he crossed the ruined grove where the Giant King had skinned and eaten the matriarch. Walks-like-a-Rockslide touched the pieces with the tip of his trunk, seeking the comfort and connection of his people's bone-ritual, and felt hollow. There wasn't nearly enough left. He'd felt the real thing a few precious times, when encountering other mammoths' bones on his travels, or as a boy under Grass-Whisper's care. Touch the bones, caress them, and know the lost one: the bone-ritual of the Blue Ochre People. He could have used such comfort now.

Probably for the best, though. Comfort, like guilt, would blunt his purpose.

A distant, muted, colossal thud tore his eyes from the sight. Raised in these hills and plains, he knew the sound of a great giant walking.

There in the misty hills: tall and lean, human-shaped, wearing a single massive pelt around its hips: a pelt painted blue. The Giant King, greatest of his kind, commanded magic as terrible as Grass-Whisper ever had in her wilder days. Perhaps, by skinning her, he'd stolen her power and doubled his own. He massed five times as much as Walks-like-a-Rockslide, and carried an oak-trunk club that could shatter a mammoth's bones. His great hands still dripped with blood.

Walks-like-a-Rockslide came up on his back legs, trunk high, and trumpeted fury. Grief. Guilt. An oath of vengeance without compromise or mercy.

The Giant King strode into the cloud-veiled crags and never looked back. He had, no doubt, heard all this before.

* * *

Rest was betrayal, but Walks-like-a-Rockslide learned that mourning drained his blood like human spears. Moody clouds hid the comfort and wisdom of the stars, and the chase had ranged beyond familiar hills: he was lost. His only guidance came from the giant's slow, heavy footfalls, and even those had stopped for the night.

Each step was a conscious effort. Press on in the dark, and he might kill the giant in his sleep—or break his leg in a ravine and lose his chance. Better to sleep just a little, guilt or no guilt, and be stronger for it in the morning.

The giant had walked between hills or simply strode over them. The next time Walks-like-a-Rockslide found a footprint, the giant's weight had squished soil up on all sides to reveal bedrock. A cold bed, but the hummocks of earth at the edge of the footprint would cut the breeze. Walks-like-a-Rockslide curled up in the footprint, trusting his pelt to keep him from freezing. He'd rested in worse places.

Perhaps he slept, perhaps he didn't; the clouded stars offered no sense of how much time had passed when the humans attacked.

The ambush took a familiar shape: a net of ropes they'd made or stolen from the Blue Ochre People. Mother had made ropes like that, even the cords that bound the great quartz blades to Walks-like-a-Rockslide's tusks. Startlement turned to fury as he smelled ochre, blood, and mammoth-hair.

These weren't the friendly traders and villagers of the Longwalkers, the Great Antler Hills, the Barde Coast. Nor were they his great enemies, the proud riders of the plains, who'd never try such a cowardly ambush. These were hill-bandits, scavengers in the wakes of giants.

He lurched to his feet. The net tugged and groaned: they'd lashed it to, what, the bases of the nearest scraggly trees? A nuisance, but then again, the point of the net was just to foul him up for the real attack.

He needed to move off this spot. Immediately.

A swipe of his stone-bladed tusks ripped at the net. Trees ripped from the earth, and anchor-ropes snapped like whips. As he hauled himself out of the giant's footprint, stone grated on stone, then escalated to a rumbling clatter. They'd triggered a rockslide, and he was moving straight toward it. Charging, even. They'd outsmarted him.

Too late to turn and run, and knowing that the front of the rockslide would shatter his legs if he set his stance, he reared up roaring against the tide of rocks and dust. His timing needed to be exact, but he knew his body, knew ambushes like this.

As rocks surged under him, he came down in front and kicked up in back. The last tumbling debris crashed against his planted front legs, and boulders scraped and punished his back legs, which he couldn't get up high enough. But the rockslide ebbed, the worst of it passed, and the rest bounced painfully, but harmlessly, off his shins. He strode through, shaking off the net and the settling dust with contempt.

And speaking of things that deserved contempt—

Here they came, ragged hill-bandits, charging into the dust-cloud with spears high. The first steps of their practiced ambush had failed, and they didn't know it yet. Walks-like-a-Rockslide felt a certain grim amusement at that, but mostly fury at the delay. A deep thud carried through the ground: somewhere, the Giant King had started walking again.

Thrown spears tangled in his fur, barely pinpricks. Others hissed past his notched ears as he turned to face the charge. One throw struck his forehead squarely: the flint spearhead crunched and fractured against the dense bone, and a hot rivulet of blood fountained down the base of his trunk. He set his stance, got his traction, and charged.

Perhaps in the dark they hadn't seen the well-used stone blade bound to each of his tusks. Their trap would have worked against most of the Blue Ochre People, but not a seasoned warrior. At the proper moment, he wrenched his head just right, wiping his right tusk-blade across their charge at the height of a human's waist. Too high to leap above, too low to duck beneath.

Battle had blunted the quartz, but anger and will had edges all their own. The long quartz blade ripped messily through two bandits and threw their ruin into their comrades. Humans fell in a tangle of flimsy limbs, too broken to shriek. Rather than ease their deaths, Walks-like-a-Rockslide whirled toward another group of spearmen. Arrows were coming down from the hills now, for all the good it would do them.

Bone crunched as he curled his scarred trunk around the legs of a warrior and hoisted him off the ground. The man—the club, now—screamed. Briefly.

Spears jabbed at Walks-like-a-Rockslide's flanks and hindquarters. He left off pounding bandits into the earth and flung his messy club sidelong to clear an archer off a ledge. As he turned, the remaining men drew back. Too many had spent their weapons on his thick fur, which was matted with stone dust, blue ochre, and many kinds of blood.

Distant, hard to feel in the earth, the giant's footsteps moved farther away. Walks-like-a-Rockslide trumpeted out his frustration and broke from the wreck of the ambush.

A spear sank home, cold and deep enough to rock him back from his course. It took him far too long to realize that the spear was in his left eye. The darkness had just seemed too natural on this gloomy night. There was pain, but he was used to pain: the wrongness of it, the intrusion, was what shocked him. He tossed his head in confusion and the spear wobbled in agonizing ways.

As more spears jabbed at his legs, he fought back panic and gripped the spear with his trunk, right where it entered his face. He steeled himself and ripped it out. It came free as if he'd torn out some unnatural growth, slick with blood and the fluid of an eyeball.

He shifted his grip to the sensitive, delicate end of his trunk and threw that spear back the way it came.

Though humans and their clever little hands could always outmatch Blue Ochre People for dexterity, he'd thrown a spear any number of times, clumsily but with enthusiasm. Losing his eye baffled his sense of distance and wrecked his aim. The spear slashed past its owner into the dark; the flailing butt-end of it cracked uselessly against the human's arm. Walks-like-a-Rockslide shuffled that way and ripped off the arm in question with a swipe of his tusk-blades.

As the bandit fell to his knees, Walks-like-a-Rockslide heaved himself up, then down, crushing the human into the gritty soil. Little bones crackled like pine-boughs in a fire.

When he whirled, the rest were running. His breath shuddered deep in his chest. The blood he'd taken seemed much less than the blood he'd lost. He ripped a spear from his shoulder with a wince. Other spears and arrows were still tangled in his fur, pricking at his thick skin, but he could handle those as he climbed deeper into the hills. The Giant King was farther away than ever.

The lost eye had been a fitting punishment for rest.

* * *

The Giant King's bed was a lifeless valley among peaks marked by handprints and trophies. Grass-Whisper's pelt hung from a pinnacle that Walks-like-a-Rockslide could never hope to climb.

Cold wind spiked through the place where his left eye had been. His outer wounds, at least, were numb by now.

The giant sat on a hill at the end of the valley, naked except for old blood, picking his teeth with a mammoth-rib. His deadly tree-trunk club rested across his knees. That club had been a matriarch oak in life, another rival. Another desecration.

He looked as tired as Walks-like-a-Rockslide felt. Grass-Whisper would not have died easily.

"Have you not lost enough, Sweet-Onion?" said the Giant King in human speech, in a voice whose echoes shivered snow off the peaks. "Your mother, and now your eye?"

How the giant knew that name unsettled Walks-like-a-Rockslide. No answer came to mind, or rather no reason to answer, and this place did not deserve the ancient mix of sound, dance, scent, and deep ground-rumble that made up Blue Ochre speech. Walks-like-a-Rockslide picked his way down a mountain pass that was a path. Years of traffic—from giants, and other peoples in better days—had ground the trail flat and smooth, but losing his eye threw off his sense of the slope. One stumble here, and he'd slide all the way down.

The Giant King heaved himself up off his seat, a hill piled high with boulders to form a crude throne. His knuckles popped as he raised the club in warning. Grass-Whisper's joints had sounded like that in later years, when Walks-like-a-Rockslide had deigned to visit between wanderings. The Giant King was old too, and worn down by a life of massive effort. Slow, perhaps. Though Walks-like-a-Rockslide had never fought a giant this size, he knew how humans fought mammoths. He'd need to think like a small creature challenging—harassing—a large one.

The valley, the giant's bed, offered some room to maneuver. The whole place was bare rock or smears of dirt. Nothing could grow here without being scraped away as the giant rolled in his sleep. With the club, the giant could reach the whole breadth of the valley if he crouched.

But although Walks-like-a-Rockslide knew he should be planning, coming at this problem differently and carefully, purpose was an avalanche in his chest. He found himself staring not at the Giant King or the oaken club, but the blue-ochre-painted mammoth-pelt hanging on one of the peaks at the valley's rim.

He listened for her voice, some sense that her spirit was with him, some echo of the connection he'd felt when she'd led him to touch the bones of the dead—and nothing whispered. Nothing comforted him, and that was as it should be.

He charged. Half as fast as a galloping horse but twice as fast as a human sprinting, he thundered down the valley's centerline. The Giant King set his stance and, at just the right time—like a mammoth meeting a charging human or shell-lion—swung that club in a hissing arc.

Stopping or turning aside weren't options, not charging on smooth rock. Instead, Walks-like-a-Rockslide sank down low and skidded.

Heat bit into his front and back knees and the front of his feet; he smelled burning hair as chunks of his pelt tore away. The club's gnarled end, what had been the oak-matriarch's crown, ripped gouges in his back but didn't solidly connect.

Walks-like-a-Rockslide came up off his knees and threw his head high. The dull quartz tusk-blades ripped along the inside of the giant's legs, just like an unlucky plains-rider had done to him once.

And remembering how he'd killed that rider, Walks-like-a-Rockslide scrambled aside, bending his momentum to a new course along the base of the throne-hill. The giant's foot came down with emphasis, perilously close. Blood sprayed across the vast slabs of stone that gave the throne its shape. The peaks shuddered: up high, the raw blue pelt flapped in an angry wind.

He bent his charge around the base of the hill and behind the throne, a piece of cover that could be useful.

Instead of another strike from that club, the Giant King brought up his other hand. It held a bloody mammoth-skull, both tusks broken off at the root.

The ancient bone-ritual, the connectedness and the knowing, hammered at Walks-like-a-Rockslide in a twisted and amplified form despite the distance between him and the skull. That was his mother's grief and loneliness bearing down on him in detail. Her love for him had brought her pain so many times, and miserable disappointment. When she died alone, she'd wondered where he was.

Walks-like-a-Rockslide stumbled against the side of the throne-hill. The worst of his mother's life poured down, unrelenting as a waterfall of ice. It did not end or relent. The Giant King's own sorcery let him warp the ancient ways that Grass-Whisper had guarded. Her skull would be just another trophy and weapon, like the club that had been a matriarch of the trees. Or placed on a mountain shelf and forgotten as a trinket, and Walks-like-a-Rockslide wasn't sure what would be worse.

He'd come up here, the magic told him, not to honor her but to give him a target for his hate, a target other than himself. And he knew the magic was telling the truth.

But the magic was also being selective, wasn't it, about what parts of his mother's life it forced on him. She'd laughed in unfeigned happiness as she shared dried fruit and the greenest trees with him, the last time he'd visited. He'd seen a grudging pride in her eyes as she bound the blades to his tusks with rope she'd rolled herself.

With one eye missing, the club came out of nowhere, a backhand swing. The oaken crown smashed him against the side of the throne. Broken, ground-down branches broke skin, sank in, cracked his ribs. He coughed out a roar and backed up around the throne-hill.

The giant planted a hand on the back of the throne and leaned over, leering down. Decades of blood darkened his gray beard. Each tooth could have been one of the great chunks of tusk he'd left behind. He'd probably eaten Grass-Whisper in a few eager bites once he ripped off her pelt.

Walks-like-a-Rockslide ran. Wild visions came to mind: charging up the side of the valley, slamming his head against the base of the peaks until the rocks rolled down to cover them both and the pelt fell free. Instead he lurched down the hill and charged.

Guilt was a distraction, and an intentional one on the Giant King's part. Grief was a distraction. The comfort of death was a distraction. His mother would want him to win, and she would want him to live. If he was being honest with himself—he'd come up here to die as much as to kill.

He drew back his trunk and lowered his head. His curved tusks slammed into the giant's right ankle. The forward points of the quartz blades punched in, not deep but enough for purchase, enough to anchor the strike. The force of the impact rocked Walks-like-a-Rockslide all up his spine. Agony drove deep into his left eye.

A return strike would come soon, but he threw caution to the wind, ripped the blades free, and swung like a human chopping a tree. Dull quartz ripped through the giant's skin and grated on the bones of the ankle.

The Giant King screamed. The noise punched into Walks-like-a-Rockslide's skull like spikes in his ears and his missing eye. He sidestepped and swung again, hooking with the tip of his right tusk. The scarred ivory point sank in behind the tendon on the back of the ankle, a cord as thick as the tusk.

And tore through.

Ivory and quartz lurched free in a gout of blood that sprayed higher than a mammoth's head. The giant fell slowly. Wind whistled in shaggy hair, in that bloody beard. By the time the giant's head cracked against naked stone, Walks-like-a-Rockslide had pivoted and shook the ringing from his ears.

Now he spoke, in the gestures and postures and words that made up the speech of his people.

<I've been selfish,> he said, <to dwell on what I feel and why I came. Perhaps killing you will comfort me, but I doubt it. What matters is this: you will kill no more elders.>

Perhaps the Giant King understood, perhaps not. The giant shook his head, slow as skidding clouds, and started to rise.

Walks-like-a-Rockslide reared up and came down on the giant's ankle with his full weight, heavy even for a mammoth. Bone cracked and grated like rock.

Grass-Whisper's skull tumbled from the giant's fist in pieces. The sight spiked grief into Walks-like-a-Rockslide's heart, but he dragged the largest pieces and the oak-trunk far out of the giant's reach, to the edge of the valley.

The work progressed from there. Quartz tusk-blades chopped into the soles of the feet, the sides of the knees, as the giant fought for purchase on smooth bloody rock.

The Giant King gripped a stony ridge and pulled himself away, and Walks-like-a-Rockslide followed implacably, swiping at whatever he could reach. Huge hands stayed out of reach, or he'd have crushed the fingers too.

Blood surged sluggishly along the base of the valley, ankle-deep for a mammoth. Sloshing through the giant's gore sapped effort like nothing else so far. Once the threat was well and truly gone, Walks-like-a-Rockslide backed away.

He'd lost the pieces of the skull, he realized. The few chunks he found, fishing in the blood with trunk and tusks, were so small and so defiled as to offer little comfort. These fragments were no true memorial, no more than the fragments of tusk had been, back at the place where she died.

In the end, Walks-like-a-Rockslide dragged himself up the smooth path where he'd entered the valley. Each slippery step took his full effort, as if saving no strength for the next step. When he succeeded in reaching the top of the pass, it came as a surprise.

Wind blasted him, turned bloody grime to dark frost in his fur as he paused to look back at his handiwork. The Giant King slumped against the side of the valley, surrounded by a lake of blood that rippled as he trembled. The oak-tree club bobbed and twisted in the blood, just out of one huge hand's reach, as if taunting its murderer.

High overhead, torrential wind caught Grass-Whisper's pelt and unfurled it like a sheltering wing, a comfort that welcomed everyone whether they deserved it or not. Unsure if he felt relief or shame or anything but pain, Walks-like-a-Rockslide sighed and turned away.

Down in the valley, the giant sighed too, and went still.

Champions Against the Maggot King

By K.H. Vaughn

The plain is vast and the mountains distant. A village stands here, empty of all souls save our troop. We line up by our Sergeant before the holes burrowed in the ground where shrines once stood. Sorrow Mai, with her horned helm, her spiked gauntlets, and her leather cuirass boiled in blood, stands at the mouth of the warren. Her axe is massive, and she wields it with both hands. She leads from the front, always, and we love her for it. The screams and hooting sounds from below echo in the tunnels beneath our feet; the earth vibrates with a dull thrum from their drums as they surface. We hold down the fear. But if Sorrow carries any fear, there is no sign.

The monsters howl as they come, filthy rags and skins strung over their furry hides, their elongate forms cruel parodies of humanity. Thin lips peel back in rage from fangs set in narrow, canine faces; their claws clutch scavenged, battered weapons. Sorrow digs her feet into the hard-packed earth and swings her heavy axe as the wave breaks upon us. Ghouls lunge at her. They claw and bite at her. They scream as the great axe cleaves their flesh. Setting her shoulders, she swings the double-headed blade in a broad arc, driving back the foes to give us room. Blood and meat spatters across the ground. I stand to her left, so that I can shield her; I work my sword, again, and again, my good shoulder popping and crackling.

We yield ground in the center, pulling them in while our flanks add to the wall of bodies. The ghoul chieftain emerges from a black hole in the ground and screams his defiance. He towers above his kind, taller than most men, taller even that Sorrow. He wears a breastplate of crudely beaten iron. A human face, stretched and cured, masks his own. His golden eyes glitter ferally within. Sorrow tears the spike of her axehead from the eye of one of his kinsman and steps to meet him. In a moment, he lies broken in the churned muck and the remaining ghouls break and retreat into the earth.

Sorrow shakes gore from the head of her axe and takes off her helmet, revealing that the ram's horns spiraling from it are her own, each curling out from the long hair that crowns her skull. She is tainted by a fiendish bloodline—a true fellborne—but we do not care. She is our champion.

Take your knife. Cut away the grease and age and wear from a copper penny until you reveal the pure bright metal beneath. That is the color of her hair.

We stride to the mouth of the warren. A foul carrion reek wafts up, and we hear the sounds of cries and baying echoing in the darkness. There will be more ghouls, and somewhere deep in the dark a nursery, where human children huddle blind amongst gnawed bones, trained to sorcery and cannibalism until their physiognomy begins to change. It is something in the blood of the ghouls—too weak to propagate themselves, they pass their curse along through kidnapping and mad ritual alone. There is no cure.

"Sergeant, if you want us to follow you down into that hole, we will," I say. I am tired from the pounding on my shield, and the work of slaughter. The rush of combat drains us all. Sorrow evaluates us as we tend the wounded and stab the enemy upon the ground to be sure they are dead. She counts the battle flags upon our backs. Her eyes burn.

"Best to kill as many as you can once you find the nest," she says. "There will be more next time."

"Then we'll always have work," I say.

She snorts a grim laugh. The ghouls are in league with the Maggot King, but this was not our mission.

"Tend to the warriors, Grath," she says. "Bring up liquid fire and that damned wizard. We'll burn out the rest as best we can."

A column of flame rises to the sky as we board our landships, and the captains order them on toward the mountains. Two score ships ride forward on thick stone slabs that undulate across the ground like the feet of enormous snails. Deep in the hulls, Dwarven earthshapers chant and beat their drums while the elementals trapped within scream in rage and pain.

* * *

Sorrow Mai strides into the hall and shoulders her way through the press of soldiers to the low table. She is broad and tall, with the heavy frame of an axe-wielder. We look at her expectantly.

"What news Sergeant?" I say.

"Captain says word has come from the Sinking City. The Emperor requires we press on against the Maggot King."

"Reinforcements?"

She shakes her head, the lamplight gleaming along the curve of her horns.

"Surely the elves," someone protests.

"No," she says. "The One Tree of Tanith rots from within and the elves wither and die with it. They look only inward. We are alone."

She sits, takes an offered mug.

"Let the elves go to rot and dust," another says. "We shall go to glory." And we cheer. Sorrow nods, approving. Our army is great and our warriors strong.

* * *

We lose another ship, the *Nanpoul*. A mass of talons and mouth-riddled tentacles rise up beneath it, grappling the hull. We watch helplessly as the souls on board slash and fire at the fleshy mass ripping their walls and tearing at their high pagodas. Impossibly, an arm the size of a great tree recoils and falls, but this is the only victory. The hull cracks with a terrible shriek and dies. A huge gout of elemental fire erupts from the keel and the thing itself collapses, its corpse now pinned beneath the weight of the shipwreck. The ship lists, broken. Smoke gives way to flame and the survivors make what escape they can. We pray a speedy death for those trapped inside. Creatures of name should not die this way. No creature should. Five thousand souls embarked aboard the *Nanpoul*. The fleet stands to take on survivors. I stand at Sorrow's shoulder, watching the wreck burn.

Pour molten steel from the forge, that amber sparking fire. That is the color of her eyes.

* * *

A scattering of souls from the *Nanpoul* come aboard late in the evening and enter the mess, swords forged from parts of the

Empire I have never seen. Ordinary swords at first, but then two more enter and the room goes silent, then collapses into whispers.

"My god, it is the Raven, Ilhar. The elf who never smiles."

"He is death. He will kill us all."

The elf wears black leather and mesh, tightly wrapped around his frame beneath a gray cloak. His skin and hair are as shadow on alabaster and his eyes black as pitch. Seeing him chills me. Indeed, I believe that if he wished it, we would all die. Only Sorrow would be strong enough to stand against him. His sword is legendary.

His companion is no less feared. The dwarf wears leather and iron over his loins and forearms, but little more, and his skin is the color of slate, except for the scars covering his body. The left side of his bald head is a riot of keloid in purple and red, burned by fire or acid. His left eye is gone, the socket covered by a bit of iron screwed into the skull. His black beard bristles like a chimney-sweep's brush. He wears his war chain wrapped around himself. He stands not quite five feet tall, a mass of knotted muscle on muscle, like an ancient walnut burl. Ko-Mon The Heartless is a ball of hate, rage, and pain. He, too, is death. The smell of urine taints the air now.

Sorrow Mai stands and says, "Ko-Mon, you are still alive? It can be from spite alone."

He smiles broadly, and the scars on his face crinkle.

"Sorrow Mai, as I live and breathe. This is the boat to die on if you are here."

"Ilhar," she says.

The elf nods, a greeting between equals. One forgets that in other circles, people speak of Sorrow Mai in whispers. But she is ours, and now these two killers are ours as well. Yet, we will still fear them, at least a little.

* * *

Beer and food, and the common bath helps. There is so much heat from the elemental engines in the bowels of the ship that we have mineral baths. It soothes weary bones, and I am thankful for it. Rank and legends become less important as we tell tales, naked but for our scars. And if we will eventually die, we can at least wash the stink of fear and butchery off our skins between battles.

Ko-Mon and Sorrow trade stories, steam coiling around them, while the rest of us listen, rapt. Some others contribute. Scars are listed and explained. I tell of the time I lost my hand, although it is a small story and no great deed. A troll struck my shield and split it in two, destroying my hand with it. Few enough have been struck down by a troll and lived to tell about it.

"Careful with the hand you have left, Grath," Ko-Mon says. "Lose that, and who will wipe your ass?" He is joking and serious at the same time, and we all laugh loudly.

Ilhar says nothing. Of all of us, Ilhar owns the fewest scars. They say he is impossible to touch with a blade; they say he plucks arrows from the air, if you can believe it. He is painfully thin, as most elves are, and the runes of his people cover his skin, row upon row of tiny sigils, like spiderwebs. His eyes are closed, but his ears twitch like those of a cat. We are laughing and content, but he is still. I am emboldened somewhat by drink.

"Ilhar," I say. "I cannot read elvish runes. Can I ask what they say?"

"These are the names of the dead that I have killed." He does not move or open his eyes. "One day, I will die. If death is kind, my skin will be taken and displayed in a place of honor. One can hope for no more than a beautiful death. One becomes more than death if death is art."

"Once I watched Ilhar duel another of his people," Ko-Mon says. "They fought for days, for each time one had advantage, the moment would not have been beautiful enough to honor the other. In the end, Ilhar found his moment, and his foe's blood sprayed across the floor."

"I loved him dearly," Ilhar says. "No one has loved another more intensely than I did him in that moment. It was a great gift he gave to me, and I to him."

A good death. One can hope for no more than that in this life.

* * *

The dragon comes in through the low clouds, weaving in and out of hiding as it approaches the ships. It swoops in low over the ship to port, unleashing a torrent of ichor that makes the ship shudder and scream. Fire and cannon-shot lash back; arrows and lances prick its back and wings. It makes no sound except the horrid wet flapping of its wings.

Aboard ship there is a shouting, fearful energy as we line up in preparation. The captain will order the gunners wait until the last moment. The archers and lancers ready for the next volley. None of it may matter against the beast's hide. Against a dragon of any age, the weapons of those who walk the earth mean little.

It flies straight on, making no effort to evade. It is so large that it seems slower than it is. Its mass fools the eye. Who has seen such a thing before and lived?

The guns roar and tear at the thing, but on it comes. Arrows fly.

We can now see the rot. The dragon is bloated with decay, like a corpse pulled from the harbor after weeks submerged. It swoops in low, and vomits up a flood of caustic putrefaction that liquifies those caught within. Now our ship writhes in pain, and no one can keep footing. A lancer falls from the pagoda above me to the deck with a scream that ends in a wet crump, her head dashed open on the stone.

The dragon drips adipocere from its many wounds as it passes overhead; we vomit and choke on the stench. It splatters huge clumps of rot and decay across the deck and walls. It clots in our mouths and lungs, suffocating us. The beast continues along the line, attacking each ship in turn, then wheels in the sky in a great lazy arc. I can hear Sorrow screaming orders, readying us for the next attack. She calls, and we answer with a scream of defiance, line up to meet our doom.

It arrives.

The dragon flies low, nearly dragging its ponderous form across the ground, then rises up and grasps the hull, tearing at the towers of the ship. The stench of rot makes warriors pass out, or stagger insensate. Tooth and claw and enormous wings batter us. The ship will be lost.

A single chain, covered in spikes and razors, lashes forth and wraps around the dragon's neck. I do not know what magic allows it to grow so long. Ko-Mon's choking grasp drags the beast's head toward the deck and there is Ilhar, who strips the rotting flesh from the back like a fishmonger fileting a salmon. The beast makes no sound, only claws and pulls away in desperation. Sorrow Mai launches herself from the tower and brings her axe down over her head into the monster's skull, and the thing shudders with a great groan. We prick at it with spears and arrows and tiny stabs as it lets go the side of the ship and collapses to the ground in a twisted heap of decayed flesh. The ulcerated, clouded eyes do not change, but it moves no more.

* * *

Elementalists struggle with the ship, for its wounds are serious. The caustic ichor of the dragon scarred it deep, and the twisted remains of warriors are melted into the stone. Our ship only knows pain. We must wait until it heals before pressing forward. They drive it away from the corrupted flesh of the dragon but it will not go far. They climb like monkeys along the parapets and walls, breathing life and soothing words into the stone as we count our dead.

"Fighting the dead," Sorrow says. "It is a losing proposition."

"I saw the final blows fall," I say. "Your legends will pass forward well beyond your death, so long as there are tongues to speak and ears to hear."

"Grath," Ko Mon says. "Do you know the tale of Damien Bloodthorne?"

"All do. He slew the Giant at Allwreck with his sword, and his brother the assassin as well. It broke his heart to do so."

"I am here to tell you that the Giant was just a man. A tall man, to be sure, but he was not twenty feet tall. No more than a head taller than Sorrow. And his brother died of syphilis, raving about angels at the asylum at Khut."

I look at him, and see that his left hand is a claw, burned like his arm and face. His face is hard to read, for I can only see the side with scars and no eye.

"Am I to believe you, or the legends? You are a legend yourself. That calculus is beyond me."

"Ha!" he said. "I like this one, Sorrow. We graybeards must stick together. Enough of him, and I could murder the Emperor himself, God rest his fucking soul."

The elementalists cut away portions of the rampart and a tower that is too far gone. The stones collapse in a heap, now lifeless, half a mile or so from where the dragon lies in ruin. The dragon lived after death, and the stone was dead matter given life, but all the parts left behind feel no more pain. I do not know where life begins and ends, but it seems the same way with us. Ko-Mon's flesh has been burned with the necrotic acid of the dragon. More scars will form upon his flesh. There is magic to build up walls, give life to dust. But knitting flesh eludes us. It heals as it will. For all his rage and pain, I feel comfortable in his presence. I believe that in his heart, he is a good being, although he would probably kill me if I were to speak it aloud.

"Your chain. It cuts your hands."

"Yes. This one," he holds up his left hand, the fingers fused by fire into a hook, "it does not bother me. But my right." He holds it up, and it is a latticework of scars upon scars. "I bleed every time I wield it. That is the cost. It feeds on pain, this chain. Pain drives it to be six feet one moment, and sixty feet another. I must admit, if I lose my right hand, I will be in trouble."

"Who will wipe your ass then? Ilhar?" I say.

"Ha! I doubt it. As my friend, he would offer to kill me. He does not think as other souls do. It is all he knows. But if it came to that, he would make it pretty. Me, I don't care how pretty death is, but I could not deny him his effort to bring me honor."

"He is quiet, that elf."

"Be thankful. I once asked him to tell me a story, and he did. I pray to every god that has ever been, and every god that hasn't, that he never tells me another."

* * *

When the fleet resumes movement across the plain, we leave eight wrecks in our wake. Again, we fold the warriors into the ranks as best we can. Some stay behind to tend the dead. Others simply cannot continue, and a trickle of broken souls walk across the plain along the broad furrows left by our passage. I have seen warriors fall upon their sword, and others simply sit down and wait to die. We all have our breaking point. I hope I do not live to see mine, but there is no shame in it.

The plain is barren, and there are no villages now. Ahead, there is only the mountain range, growing slowly larger in the distance. The Maggot King's keep is there. There will be warrens filled with horror and death beneath. They may extend so deep within the earth that there is no end to them.

A wave of wild men break against the ship. They are pathetic. Pale and soft, but secure in their sense of power, waving their genitals at us as they come. They howl in impotent rage as they die, mowed down by arrows and lances. The ship rolls over them and churns their corpses into the dirt. No one will find their bones or mourn their deaths. Where does the Maggot King find them? There must be thousands of them in the dim light of subterranean caves, thinking of nothing but their eventual victory.

Sorrow watches this display of manhood impassively.

"Do you think they die with pride, as we would, to die for our cause?" I say.

"I do not care. They made their choice, to throw themselves against a millstone. There is nothing that they can do, expending their lives against us like this. It is stupidity, not honor."

"But are we different?"

"Who can say? We were never meant to win this fight. The Emperor does not care if we defeat the Maggot King. He only cares that we deplete our strength so none can rise against him."

"That cannot be. Surely we are in the right?"

"The Maggot King is evil. That does not mean that the Emperor is good. Either way, our forces will be spent, and the Emperor remains on his sinking island with his drug-addled wife. Grath, you are brave and loyal, but what do you fight for?"

I look to the evening sky. Since we left upon this journey, we have been harassed by faceless, rubbery creatures that attack by night. They swoop in and steal away those on watch. It is difficult to spot them until you hear the screams. Sometimes they drop their victims, well after they are taken. They are frozen to the core. I always believed that it was warmer, the closer one came to the sun, but I now know that is not true.

"Sergeant, I confess that I no longer know what to believe."

"When I was small, maybe eight years old, I became ill with a fever. An itinerant priest brought me back. There was no heaven waiting, only darkness. I don't know if that is for everyone, or only for my kind. That is what I know. That I know nothing beyond what is before me now."

"That can't be all. This much pain and death. It must mean something. There must be something greater that we serve."

"That may be. I only know what I know."

"I do not understand the strategies of the Maggot King. We are now a dozen ships, no more than sixty-thousand swords among the souls riding across the land. He sends his forces piecemeal against us. There is no order in his actions. Ghouls, the Deep Worm, the dragon, men, demons from the night sky. Send them all at once and he could break us."

"Perhaps he himself is unable to muster such coordinated effort. Perhaps the energy of staying alive alone is as much as he can manage. In any case, we will face him, and more will die."

It is not much to go on, without belief in something. It is to my shame that I cannot tell her why I fight. It is for my comrades. It is for her.

* * *

Cannons fire at the walls of the enemy outside his mountain keep. Magic fire rains down from trebuchets. His outer ramparts are ancient stone in poor repair, impressive only by virtue of scale. The bombardment lasts for days and the dust of rock and bone seeps into our pores. The Maggot King does little to oppose us, secure deep within the earth, so we must go to him. Sorrow, Ilhar, and Ko-Mon will lead the charge. So many legends. Will it be enough against the Maggot King?

When it is time to arm ourselves, my comrades strap my shield to my arm and I take my place at my Sergeant's side. As her second, I will protect her as best I can. The ramps drop, and we surge forward, a press of desperate flesh against the steel and talons of the enemy. He is buried deep. We will dig him out.

He sends all manner of abomination against us. Constructs of flesh and bone, men driven mad with rage and lies. We slip on the blood, ours and theirs. It pools and runs in rivulets down the slope in the passageways, ever downward. The body holds a gallon or more. The gallons drain, become a river. Somewhere in the deep, I imagine there will be pools deep enough to drown in.

We fight our way deep into the halls of the Maggot King. The sun has never seen the places where good swords die. Most of us will be forgotten and go unnamed. We are numbers. Bones that become dust.

The hall of the Maggot King is something to behold. It is a vast place of polished stone, shaded between ivory and obsidian. Great pillars extend far out of sight to a ceiling that we cannot see. Motes of sickly green light float erratically around us, creating strange shadows. Bodies hang from hooks and chains, and rot in iron cages. From somewhere high in the darkness, a cascade of blood, collected from the rivers of it spilled above, crashes down like thunder. It is a mile to his throne, and a host of degenerate beings stand between him and our forces. They howl and beat their shields and hammer the floor with iron.

But now, they charge, and blood sprays darkly in the thin light. The first wave rides upon toads large enough to swallow a man whole, and the sight of a human hand pressing frantically against their terrible gray skin like that of a babe in the womb fills me with dread. My arm grows tired from stabbing. I see the light go from the eyes of my enemies, the tears of fear and disbelief as they realize they are dying. Truly, his last guardians thought they were immortal. Beside me, Sorrow's axe swings back and forth, leaving behind a trail of heads and limbs until there is a lull and her broad shoulders slump ever so slightly with fatigue. I am exhausted, trembling and afire with pain. Halfway down the hall, the next wave of the enemy arrives. They move with a strange lurching gait, and I am sure that whatever they were in life, they are now in various stages of decay. Some men, some trolls, some giants even, by the size of them. I sheath my sword a moment so that I can fumble open a horn to drink. Thus, I am unarmed when the ambush comes.

They boil from out of hidden doors in the walls, hundreds of them in our ranks at once, swinging their clubs and axes blindly.

44

These too were once men, but their flesh is desiccated and they break like dry wood. They grab my empty hand and wrestle me, pressing my arm back and up. Then fire burns my gut, punctured again and again with ferocity. As they let me fall to the floor, Ilhar is there, and he dances in and out of our intermingled ranks with impossible speed. I watch, amazed, as he drifts among them, cutting, slicing. In this moment, I am enthralled by the beauty he creates. I understand his philosophy of art and death, if only for a short time. These creatures do not deserve the glory he has given them.

When it is over, I myself am broken on the stone floor of the hall of the Maggot King. Sorrow stands over me. There is sadness in her eyes. Magic can bind that which has no life, but not living flesh. My insides are torn and my chest sucks and gurgles. I cannot feel my legs.

"Not looking so well, my friend," she says.

"You go on ahead, Sorrow. I'll catch up when I can. Save a few of them for me."

"As your friend, I will end your life, if that is your wish," Ilhar says. It is the kindness he knows.

I smile and shake my head. Ilhar nods and flits away.

Ko-Mon touches my face, tenderly. There are tears on his face.

"You have done well, my friend. Your story will be told."

And he too is gone. A flood of swords and lancers follow. Sorrow Mai lingers a moment.

"I am sorry to lose you, old friend. I hope you find your paradise across the river." She turns away, broad back and horned helm. If anyone will strike a blow against the Maggot King, or against the Emperor himself, it will be her.

Polish rust until it is smooth and bright and clean. That is the color of her skin.

Now that she is gone, I admit I love her as more than a sergeant. But that does not matter now. I lie in the dwindling light amongst corpses and listen to the screams of the dying and of the dead. My war is over.

The King's Two Bodies

By Joe Koch

We are kings under the skin

Where the visible and invisible bodies meet

In creamy shadow, curvature of bone,

Cleft below forward shoulder,

Clavicle backed by strong meat.

The true king wears the skin of many men,

Swears the oaths of his kind, draws tight

The knot on sloping bone; the bow made from remains

Of old kings. He guards the secret haunted body

Below the mountain of a symmetrical chest,

Landscape of pulse and neck.

Thus the true king revokes his eyes

To mime mere flesh.

Color pours from his broken sockets, floods the cup

At the root of his throat. Between clavicle wings,

The king's two bodies pool over a sternum calling

Buried kings back from the land's lost history.

Tongues search the cup where his throat dips into hiding,

Sip the liquid drum of his seen and unseen pulse.

The symmetry of the visible body reveals

Rivals crowned within.

Curved tongues fit the concave dent

And taste the banner of a man's armored breast.

Fingertips crack open the curve down his back,

Draw tight the bow-strung collarbone and take

Aim at pretenders. The liquid invisible king surges

Around the arrow thrust down his throat.

Let tendons tremble. Take his skin, his crown,

His ring, his cloak. His hair, his eyes, his colors,

His bones. Unearth the bloated dead born

Of mortified fat and bleed the king's two bodies

Below the knots of disingenuous veils and forced dress.

Breed freedom from the cup of clean bones.

Stitch riven flesh where the seen and unseen meet;

Raise the bow high, and hold, hold.

The Origin of Boghounds

By Amelia Gorman

Boghounds are a curious creature, and everyone seems to have a different story about their birth. I've heard someone say if you take a whelping mutt to the swamp under a full moon and cut her open with a wooden knife, the runt will be a boghound. Others say they're the ancestral dogs of the Mandrakes, hunting the world in search of a substitute for their extinct masters. Or, they're simply an exaggerated variation of the web-toed birding spaniel. One of the less likely stories says they're what comes out when a heeler mates with an alligator.

They'll sleep on your feet in front of the fire like a regular dog; they'll sit and heel and bark too. But no one knows how they walk through the muck like it was no more than a thick fog beneath their feet. No one knows if they breathe underwater, or if their lungs just hold enough air to last them an hour or more. They'll lick your hand, they'll come when called, and then they'll eat a poisonous snake like it was nothing at all. The most common way to see them is as part of a whole team, pulling a sledge with an Arum forager at the back. Sometimes swimming, sometimes splaying their webbed feet across the slippery bog bottom, the pack slides packages of angelica and peat, cresses and cranberries, black tubers and medicinal mummy sludge into the port city of Sichel.

You came to my shop for tea, packaged and pulled by boghounds across the murk. Stay awhile, let me brew you a sample. Because I have another story about the origin of boghounds, one I don't think you've ever heard. Before I introduce you to the dog of the story, let me introduce you to the woman. Meet Samphire.

Years ago, Samphire left the fog-catching business for the man-catching business. If you don't know the dirty secrets behind the fog merchants that might seem a step down, but she found bounty hunting less dangerous and more lucrative. There's more in common there than meets the eye, too. She probably fished snotsnakes as a child. Simply put, she's a woman born to catch slippery things.

Her eyes are always open a little too round and a lot too wide, like someone who saw so much of the sun on the ocean she'll never get used to the dark. Tired pupils constantly strive to make the light right enough. But her chewed-down lips, sucker scars and white-streaked hair mark her as a person who saw too much watery death— and things worse than death that come crawling out of the sea. So she switched to hunting criminals in the bogs on the edges of Sichel, the Stained City.

* * *

On the day Samphire learns the origin of boghounds, she's hunting Glib Halb: extortionist and quacksalver. His "cures" for the Wasting White poisoned a dozen people in The Gills and the Gallows, including two children. And she has a special hatred for mountebanks.

You might at first think Glib Halb is lucky to be hunted by this little slip of a bug-eyed woman. It's a preferable situation to being slaughtered by The Boulder, or stalked by the dread Viergang, or Belladonna and her hulking lover of the week, or any of the other infamous not-quite-law of Sichel, isn't it? But Samphire's reputation is built on never bringing her bounties back alive. She has a fine talent for pickling and preservation, picked up long ago when she learned to bottle the fog. She never has problems proving the veracity of her art. Scam artists are not limited to doctors and pharmacists, of course, and a common grift in that trade is to kill any alleyway drunk and claim them as a lost murderer. Especially here in the damp, bodies decompose quickly. This makes the courts, the honest ones at least, very particular about wanting criminals brought back alive only. Unless you're Samphire, who's allowed to work her particular magic. When she brings in a head, a flayed face, or a hand with a peculiar and identifiable scar, there's no wiggle room in the provenance. Which means instead of overpowering her prey, she can hunt them with stillness and secrecy, killing them with poison or a knife in the middle of the night.

Physically, she looks like nothing so much as a great wading bird, the sort with long legs that bend in backwards ways and an elongated face and neck. The kind of bird that runs out to make its catch and instinctively turns back just before the cresting waves arrive to overtake it. Her hair is cut to a sheer, severe line along her chin and greased tightly back to let her too-wide eyes wander where they must. Bog or ocean, she always wears oiled boots up her thighs and hunches under a giant pack full of glass jars, oils, and knives. Like a snail, she burdens herself down with what she needs to make her home wherever she is.

She takes her home back and forth through the streets of Sichel, asking where to find the man who sold poison to the city. A grief-stricken stevedore holds back tears in the Gills while he explains he bought medicine for his son out of a little pharmacy on Nacrebaker street. The pharmacy is cleared out, a for-rent sign already in the window. But a few more questions, a little bit more prying, and she learns he paid a jaundiced old soak in liqueurs and herbs to box up and bring alembics, firewood, bottles and barrels to a noxious little peathouse on the edge of the bog. And yes, for just a small donation, the drunk can even sketch her a little map.

* * *

The sun sets through the weeping trees as Samphire picks her way over the muddy ground to a cabin made of turf and timber, covered in moss. One window is all it offers to the wider world, and even that is long since boarded shut as a dead man's eye. She creeps once around the outside before entering to confirm her first impression: the ingress is the egress. Then she carefully, silently, opens the door.

The light continues to disappear as dark violet clouds hasten the end of day. Herbs and strings of lacey lichen blow in the wind that enters alongside the hunter. Yellow slugs fall from the ceiling, but the house is empty of human occupants. Samphire lights a candle hoping for just a sniff of a trail.

Anything out of the mountains of bric-a-brac stacked to the ceiling could hold the little thread she grabs to continue the search. There are more shelves of books than the cabin ought to hold, blue ink diagrams nailed to the beams, bones and skulls and rocks and hagstones in tidy little piles. Flat against the back wall is a bed covered in clean straw and dirty wool. Here is the presence that has been peeking at the edge of our story from the beginning. The two precious eyes, the curious nose. Nestled into that wool is a boghound, curled in a perfect circle with her chin touching her toes and her tail wrapped tight around her body.

Samphire has seen boghounds before, but rarely and only from a distance. Cats are more common companions in Sichel, used by both boat and building to keep pests at bay. Since pests are very common, the cats grow fat and friendly. Stray dogs and pets from rich households occasionally mingle in the streets, but those are cagier. They're more likely to see danger in a stranger's hand than food or friendship. Yet every so often, a swamp trader comes through with a whole working team of boghounds. They yap and fight in packs on the plaza, lapping up spilled beers and tearing scraps from each other's mouths, bearing bloodied lips and snarling.

It feels, to Samphire, that a pack of boghounds is one wrong turn from exploding. Pulling taut, they test the control of their sledge drivers as if there was one rotten word or one poison cue that might accidentally snap and release them to wreak havoc on the city. But the words always held them fast.

This one in front of her is on the smaller end— maybe it weighs only three stone, maybe less— mostly tan with a distinguished white stripe on its head. It lifts that handsome head to look at Samphire with shining yellow eyes, yawns and licks its lips. Then, it raises itself up on those rangy, muscular legs and walks over to the intruder. The boghound licks Samphire's hand, and she reaches over to scratch it on its oily head in spite of herself. She spots a scrap of leather that lay in the straw mattress underneath the creature and picks it up with her free hand.

It's a journal. Samphire stops her affection to flip through, hunting the thread. The first page is an unmistakable sketch of this very animal, and the writing begins on the second. "I acquired a young boghound and named her Hum..." it begins.

Samphire eyes the hound. "So girl, your name is Hum, eh?" she says, and the dog gives a friendly wag of its tail in response. But there's an interruption before she can continue reading. The door creaks without quite cracking and voices waft into the cabin.

Samphire blows out her candle and slips into the dark corner between the headboard and wall. She disappears into the dark sod and crouches down into a knot in the tiny crawlspace, barely fitting with her giant pack of unguents and vinegars. Hum hops silently off the straw, pads over to her and crawls under the bed, looking up at her with those affectionate golden eyes like two stars in the dirty dark.As the dark obscures their faces, Samphire catches voices she's butted against time and again. At work, at play, and— worst of all— in the wilderness like this.

"If we get lucky, we'll catch him naked and helpless in bed." This voice is distant and seductive, like an oil painting of a waterfall.

"You'd like that, wouldn't you?" This one tinged jealous and angry, the smell of coming thunder.

The first is Belladonna, the second is Canner, and both are competition. There's uneasy peace in the city. After all, these three are extensions of the law itself. It's no good for them to brawl or mug each other like common criminals. How thin those lines are from time to time, though. Maybe some of those we trust would betray us. Maybe some of those we malign deserve better.

But there is no truce for them in the wilderness.

Canner lights a torch, and Belladonna spews a frustrated sigh at the seemingly empty cabin. Another shower of snails falls down, and she brushes one off Canner's shoulder. His old loose-knit shirt is drilled to scraps by moths. A sword at her waist is all rusty steel and nicked edge, almost as much not there as it is there. They are down on their luck, desperate and dangerous. The flickering torchlight reveals gaunt, ragged faces.

"Doesn't matter anyway. Air is cold, fire's out. No one's been here in at least a day."

"Tear the place apart anyway," Canner says, eager to turn his disappointment into destruction.

It's no time at all till they find her in the corner. She's trapped, fewer knives and fewer legs than her rivals. She still has a trick or two in that giant snail-pack of hers, though. Quiet as ice, she pulls the most flammable preserving oil from her bag. It's swamp gas, and a strong fermented liqueur from those black tubers that are rumored never to rot. The liquid effervesces with trapped gas bubbles and a soft hazel glow.

Nearly dislocating her shoulder, she contorts her arm back, giving herself enough room to work. There's only going to be one chance at this. She pitches the flask at the torch in Canner's hand and both explode in a fireshower. The smells of burnt hair and burnt meat collide. He falls back, screaming and knocking over a shelf full of opalescent vertebrae fossils like so many scattered marbles.

Samphire springs up and lunges for the open door where even the tenuous safety of the night is preferable to this peat shack full of smoke and violence. Rather than help her partner, Belladonna blocks the door, thirsty for vengeance.

"I should have known it would be you, you little cheat," she hisses.

That thirsty, rusty woman tackles Samphire and they both fall to the ground. A couple glass bottles shatter, but Samphire is shielded by the wads of filler in her giant bag.

Eerie blue-green foxfire illuminates the room while the orange torch gasps its last on the ground. It looks like the women are battling each other slowly in some underwater kingdom of rippling light. Belladonna kneels over Samphire, digging both her thumbs into the other woman's throat. Canner gurgles something raw and smoky-throated nearby.

A third body unexpectedly throws itself into the pile. Hum locks all her muscles like a tight little barnacle and clamps her jaws on Belladonna's arm, teeth pushing through that tender dirty flesh now slick with blood. The limb flops uselessly, no longer capable of choking Samphire. Belladonna flounders with her other arm, finally knocking the dog off herself along with a strip of skin, flapping in that fanged mouth.

Samphire is up like lightning, still clutching the book and sprinting for the door. Hum lets out a victorious howl and lopes behind her. They leave the burning cabin to run into the murk and muck together.

* * *

The same way a boghound is like a dog but not a dog, a bog is not quite a swamp. Trees grow in swamps. In fact, you can put most any plant in a swamp and it will live, at least for a while. The weak, acidic soil of bogs only grows stranger things, both prehistoric or impossibly new. Specialized things that love the peat, underwater plants that still remember the primeval lake that formed these wilds but adapted in spite of themselves.

The other difference is layers. A bog is built on countless ancient layers. Peat, then bodies, then more peat. Water, then more bodies, a final layer of peat. And all the strange gather atop it, feeding off the layers.

When she's far enough away from the house, Samphire finally removes her heavy brown bag from her back, takes out the broken glass, and lets it sink into the muck. She sits on the driest spot she can find, a porous pink rock. In the light of a small fire and the eerie luminescence of the bog, she begins to read more of the journal she found in the cabin. Hum paces in circles around the fire like some kind of protective ward.

Most of the pages contain a word or a couple of words and a brief sketch of a hand gesture, each one a common command. From this she learns Hum can heel, can come when called, can attack, and do many other things—including "Go to your Master." If there is a scent, if there is a second bolt hole or laboratory, Samphire now has a way to track it down. She's found the way to hunt Glib Halb through the bog, and Hum is happy to oblige.

* * *

This land is beautiful in its own way. Striding along with Hum just in front of her, Samphire falls into a slow, steady rhythm. First the sucking, then the squelching, as she pulls her feet in and out of the peat. Suck. Squelch. Repeat. Here or there, an easier refrain reveals itself in the form of little wooden paths used by witches, traders, and foragers.

The rich winey color of the stagnant water reminds her of burning Sichelport brandy. The carnivorous plants, sometimes large enough to consume rats and frogs, remind her a little of her friends and a lot of her enemies. Everywhere she looks there is a riot of hundreds of species, fighting for little bits of sun. They shoot out fingers, teeth, tendrils and dew-tipped needles in countless colors, shapes, and lengths.

But she is more used to following than being followed, and doesn't recognize the feeling of eyes creeping over her footsteps. She doesn't detect the motion that follows another following in the wake of wind left by her shoulders. Hum might realize it, almost certainly smells the other human scents of burned skin and bloody scab that trails behind. But Hum isn't talking.

For every step she takes towards Glib Halb, urging Hum onward with cries of "Master!" and "Wait!" when the little beast gets too far ahead, Belladonna and Canner take one of their own, not far behind her.

Through sinkholes and gaseous clouds, this land is dangerous in its own way as well. Always, the bog keeps to its own old and wild ways. To the right, a pitcher plant large enough to sink her foot into, a gallon of sticky sap inside. Some wanderers have to cut their feet off to get out of those. To the left, a shimmering drosera curls around a crow. The bird's struggle secures it tightly into that sticky club.

At one point, she cowers under a curtain of lichen, holding her breath while a giant lizard the size of a carriage trundles by. Hum buries herself almost completely in the mud, only her yellow eye sticking out, tiny silent bubbles rising and she exhales silently into the water.

* * *

But eventually they come to a little path where the ground is firmer and Samphire can keep an easy pace with Hum. Someone's feet have stalked this ground enough that the swamp grasses and thick freshwater weeds are trampled down and not getting up. In time, their pathway leads to a little grove, and that little grove is surrounded by great weeping ferns that obscure its center. Flowers littered around the outside look sick and alien even compared to the rest of the bog. A spray of cloudberries glows with amber tumors, each one encasing a seven-legged embryo. Brown ladyslippers slink to and fro of their own volition.

Samphire swats a spiral fiddlehead out of her eyes as she enters to see a perfectly circular pond in the middle of the grove. Around it, smaller greenish pools of different shapes make up a mosaic of glassy water in the land.

She bends over one, and in its emerald waters she sees a ribcage. Half a skull winks at her from beside a glittering machete. The whole thing smells toxic.

Samphire removes her bag and fishes out an empty jar to take a sample when the air trembles and a ripple starts from the center of the pool in the middle of the grove. Concentric circles travel outwards and the whole mirrored surface shudders. The ground shakes, and water in the center rips itself open like the entrance to another world. Or like an exit.

And from that other world, hell incarnate begins to rise. The torso of a woman as large as a house lifts itself, and Samphire's head cranes with it. The horror is covered in mud and scum, with snakes for eyes and moss draped like a cloak around her shoulders. Black hair cascades over her back and chest like an avalanche of void. The rest of her is naked and glossy and risen up to her waist. The giantess opens her toothless mouth to croon something deep, primal, and nearly soothing. Soothing, if it weren't coming from a mouth a man could walk through like a door.

Half-tentacle, half-sundew appendages climb up with her, dozens of them thick as arms. In the end, she has no shortage of teeth, hers are just in all the wrong places, scattered over these extremities like a monster from the sea. Samphire freezes but Hum just bows and wags her tail playfully in front of a tentacle. It prods the air around the dog, zipping to and fro like a firefly.

In that agonizing hell-moment while the monster rises up like a second sun before her, Samphire feels cold metal poke her ribs from behind. So this is it, she thinks, and wonders which saint blessed her with a quick death instead of slow mastication by those pink pink gums.

Canner's voice finds its way through the horror to her ears, and she focuses her last little spark of sanity on that.

"Give us the dog and the book," he says, "and then we can see about all three of us getting out of here alive."

But how could you give away a dog that was never yours to begin with? Halb didn't give Samphire the dog. Neither strange doctor nor bounty hunter has a claim to being its master. Instead, they were both in their own time the dog's chosen companions. Which is not to say the dog is entirely masterless.

Whatever slimy underworld this giant monstrosity comes from, it's still coming. As it rises another several feet in the air it dwarfs the two hunters, turning them into miniature figures, one little doll holding a needle to the other. A grotesque mass just barely out of the pond yelps and whimpers, and those new sounds join the unearthly croon.

Attached by ropey umbilical cords are boghounds by the dozens like wet grapes on a vine. Some are young and hairless with closed eyes, others fuzzed with soft sweet coats. The ones that have started to grow fur are all orange with a single distinctive stripe down their heads. Hum has found both her master and her birth-mother in this bog.

Belladonna has been standing back, with a better view and better eyesight than her burnt and straining partner. She understands enough to shamble backwards from this new layer of horror. But as she does, her foot thrashes through one of the glittery green puddles, this one wide but barely as deep as her ankles. She keeps moving, trying to backtrack for the safety of the path and the way out and the goddamn wilderness but her foot won't obey her. She falls backwards as the rest of her body expects her stuck heels to obey, and catches herself with her hands in the puddle. Her fingers sear, red as a rare sunburn as she attempts to push herself up again and again. The barest threads on her clothes are already coming apart, leaving her in even more tattered rags that dissolve in the pool faster but just as surely as skin eventually will.

One of the sundew claws has caught a strange prickling wind on its hairs, or the scent of raw meat in the pool, or some other sign of life and tries to narrow in on Canner and Samphire. It hovers eye-level with them, probing the air like a serpent's tongue, before lunging. It knocks them both down with its ruby-fringed head. Lucky for them, they fall backwards to the soft ground instead of forwards into the verdant pool in front of them.

Before they can scramble back up, it wraps its stem around Samphire. All she can think is that its embrace is cool and sticky where she thought it would be hot and sharp. With impossible plant strength it starts to lift her off the ground and she grabs for the nearest thing to keep her on this earth. That thing is Canner. She's upside down and heading fast towards that toothless gullet, so she twists and grabs onto his thighs while both slip like mudskippers in the greasy peat.

She has an idea to save herself. "Hum! Pick it up!" she yells in one frantic final effort, her hands already losing their grip on Canner. She gestures with her chin while her fingers desperately clutch at dirty trousers. He kicks at her and wipes his eyes, spitting out a mouthful of peat.

And Hum does! That beautiful beast! Hum picks it up. She gently mouths the stem like this is all some kind of game. And it responds, tickling the dog and gently trying to extricate itself from the hound's mouth without hurting its child and servant.

Her feet are free but Canner is on her again. He punches her in the face and her eyes ring in time with the pulsing ground that still trembles with the master-of-hounds' arrival. With the dogs' slick and giant humanoid-plant mother.

One hand wrenches itself free, grabs the rusty knife lost in the tangle and sticks it into him again and again. The blood drives the tentacles wild with joy and they swarm over him in a flurry of tendrils, teeth, and sweat. They forget Samphire completely. The ring of puppies yips excitedly while she scoots back, stands and runs. As far away from the carnage as she can.

* * *

Is this the end? Not of Samphire and Hum's stories, they're both still out there. Maybe they're still together, even. If they are, I hope for their sake they are far from the bog. Maybe aboard a whaling ship, maybe loping through the dunes. Maybe for my sake, I hope they are close, and I can see my young Hum again. But it's the end of this story. And I swear it, if not entirely true, is very much like a true thing.

It is the end, or very near, of Belladonna's story. I found her later, still rotting in the digesting pool. I promised her a quicker death if she told me everything she saw. We both delivered. The rest, the details of Samphire while she's alone, I can only guess at with some creative license. Please forgive an old apothecary, an old mountebank some might say, this fun I have had imagining. I believe it is all very likely.

But this I have known for a long time as the true origin of boghounds. Sometimes they ripen and break free from their mother on their own and find their way into the world. Other times, a man whose peers called him a quack and criminal, he finds a lost little puppy in his cabin years ago. He raises it, trains, researches the older miracles of this damp earth. He finds a way to stalk and harvest its siblings from their ghoulish fields.

And though I, Halb, may train them, in the cities and in the bogs, train them to find their master. I may learn the secret way to encroach safely and cut pups off the vine. I may eventually replace the good sound boghound I lost to a bright young bounty hunter. But we are not their masters. We are at best their temporary guardians, their borrowers. Because a boghound is not a dog, and we will never be masters of such curious creatures.

Well Met at the Gates of Hell

By David K. Henrickson

The man stands upon the barren plain. Before him, a road stretches into the distance, worn into the stone by an endless procession of feet. At his back, a sheer rock wall towers into a pitch-black sky. Dust spins in fitful eddies across the hard earth, driven by a wind like the breath from a furnace. On the horizon, a city shines dimly where it clings to a vast spire of rock that climbs into the blackness until it is lost to sight.

For a moment, the man cannot remember what has brought him there.

Three figures wait for him beneath a sky that is the absence of all things. The first is a giant of a man, a head taller than the newcomer and half-again as wide. Light from the sullen fires burning upon the plain turn the plate of his armor red, the strands of his heavy beard the color of copper. His arms are corded with muscle. In one massive hand, he holds a sword no normal man can lift. It glows with a soft, unhellish light. The newcomer knows it to be the sword named *Remorse*. It is said only the pure of heart can wield it.

The second man is smaller than the newcomer, hard and lean like a bone gnawed overlong by a dog. He wears a leather jerkin and smiles a smile that holds only hatred as he considers the new arrival. His hand toys restlessly with the long dagger on his belt, the pommel a ruby the size of a hen's egg.

The third figure is not a man at all. The human has not been born who can read meaning in the faceted eyes of an insect or understand the mind behind them. The huge mantis sits upon its back two sets of legs, towering over its companions. The antennae on top of its head move ceaselessly. A soft, continuous clicking sound issues from its thorax.

The giant is the first to speak. "I told you we would meet again." A paladin whose name was once known across half the world, his voice is gentle and reserved. "Even before the Gates of Hell, there is justice."

Studying the three, the newcomer's memory begins to clear. He is dressed as he had been at the moment of his death, his face grimed with war, his armor blackened and rent from battle, the cries and the tumult of that final conflict still echoing in his ears.

It seems events had not worked out the way he had hoped. *Oh well*, he thinks. *Win some, lose some.* He might have expected to feel more outrage at his own death, but the passions of life already seem to be passing.

Just as well. He could admit to himself, here in this place, that while forging an empire had been fun, running it had been a bore. At least he had done some good. Well, a little. Mostly, there had been a lot of fighting.

The giant looks at his two companions and takes a step forward. "We have agreed mine is the prior claim. If I should fall, it will be their turn."

"Don't you ever tire of being used?" the newcomer asks the giant conversationally, hitching at a loose plate on the pauldron protecting his left shoulder.

Early in the battle, a sword thrust had nearly severed the fastenings holding it in place. It had been a nuisance all day. He had killed the man who had done it without ever seeing his face or knowing his name. Battles were like that.

"Your companions only seek to spare themselves the danger of being first," he adds. "Or to make their task easier should you fail."

"The reason does not matter," the paladin replies. "The deaths of the innocent cry out for revenge. Guard yourself." The corded arm raises the shimmering blade.

The newcomer knows it can slice through steel like flesh. He does not lift his own blade in return. Instead, he tugs at the loose plate on the pauldron again. "They weren't all that innocent," he replies reasonably. "And the case could be made that they've already been avenged. After all, look where we are."

The shining blade lowers as the giant speaks again. "There must be an accounting. Beyond the grave, if necessary."

The newcomer rolls his shoulders and stares up at the sky. There is not a single star to relieve the blackness. That could get monotonous after a while, he decides.

He thinks of the battle again. It had lasted all day, beneath clouds of ash that blotted out the sun. While the outcome might not have been everything he could have wished for, the carnage itself had been immensely enjoyable. In retrospect, even his death now gave him a sense of satisfaction. It had been a fitting climax to a life lived to the fullest.

"Poetic, but hardly realistic," he says. "You've championed enough lost causes to know the books never balance."

"Get on with it," the man with the dagger says to the giant. "He'll talk your hind legs off if you let him."

"You never did listen," the newcomer says to him. "That was always your problem."

"You were my problem," the other retorts angrily.

"Still blaming others for your own inadequacies, I see. And

letting them fight your battles. Some things never change."

The smaller man just spits.

"You cannot avoid your fate by dissembling," the giant says, stepping closer.

The newcomer appears not to notice, the sword remaining at his side. "I would say I am precisely where I am meant to be. You, on the other hand, do not belong here. Give up this pointless quest for vengeance."

"I made a vow."

"Reconsider. You know what they say about good intentions."

"I cannot."

"Will not. Surely, one life is enough to give. Why condemn yourself to endless suffering? Leave us to our just reward—an eternity in our own company. What could be more fitting than that?"

As he says this last, he steps forward himself, turning in a circle with one hand flung wide. He gestures to the pitch-black sky above, still struggling with the troublesome pauldron with the other.

Inadvertently, the giant glances up, following the other's gaze. In that moment, the newcomer skims the plate he has finally freed from his armor toward the giant's eyes and throws himself forward in a roll.

Automatically, the giant flinches away from the spinning metal. "Faithless!" he cries out, aiming a blow at the tumbling figure as it dives past.

The newcomer is already inside and below the other's guard. His blade flashes out in a backhanded swing, shearing through the giant's thigh just above the greave.

Then he is out of range, rolling to his feet smoothly and turning to face the bigger man.

"Honorless cur!" The giant hops on one foot, swaying to maintain his balance. "Worthless wretch!"

"You did say 'Guard yourself'," the newcomer says. "You should have taken your own advice."

"I will have your blood!"

"Unlikely."

"Come at me," the giant challenges, bracing himself..

"I don't think so."

The giant tries to take a step forward, incensed. His knee buckles beneath his great weight.

The newcomer merely looks on with interest. "I have all the time in the world," he says. "You, on the other hand, are at a significant disadvantage. I believe I was fortunate enough to sever the tendon. It would be better if you were to withdraw. My offer is still good. I have no quarrel with you."

"Never," the giant swears. "The dead would never forgive me."

"The dead have other things to worry about," the newcomer says. "Trust me on that."

"I will not yield."

The newcomer sighs. "Have it your way."

After that, it's just a grim, tiresome business. The giant advances, his opponent retreats, circling to take advantage of the other's injury. The paladin cannot pivot quickly enough to protect himself at all times and, even if the other man's weapon has no name, it is still wickedly sharp. Time and again, it finds chinks and crevices in the other's armor. Finally, it bites into the big man's neck.

The end comes quickly after that. The giant stumbles a final time, falls, and does not rise.

"Well, that was tedious," the newcomer says, considering his fallen foe. He looks at the others. "I don't suppose we can consider honor satisfied? Best one out of three? I don't know about you two, but I've had a long day."

The remaining man screams, draws his dagger, and charges. The newcomer just has time to brace himself.

There is a single clash of blades, then the two men crash together, spilling to the ground in a tangle of limbs. Over and over they roll, grunting and straining. When things finally settle down, the newcomer has his opponent's arms pinned behind his back, while his legs grip the other man's body fast. Under other circumstances, it might be considered a rather intimate tableau.

In his free hand, the newcomer now holds the other's dagger.

Silently, the smaller man struggles to free himself. The bigger man masters him without any real effort.

"I've always thought this blade overstated," he says, examining the weapon when the other finally grows tired. "I remember when your mother gave it to you."

The smaller man tries to head-butt him without success. "She told me to kill you with it," he says.

"And so you fail her again."

"This time. I'll be back!"

The newcomer knows it is not an idle boast. No one dies the real death in the land of the dead.

"Hush, now." And with that, he slides the dagger home—beneath the edge of the jerkin and up through the rib cage until it finds the heart.

The other spasms, a small fountain of blood spraying from his lips. The newcomer waits a moment for the thrashing to cease, then rolls the body off his legs and stands.

The mantis sits waiting, its thoughts hidden behind inhuman eyes.

"Did you enjoy that?" the man asks.

"It always pleases me to see humans kill one another," the insect says. Its voice is sharp and dry, as cold as the mind behind those eyes. Deliberately it grooms its giant, seizing claws—first one and then the other—with mandibles that can bite a grown man in half.

"You should talk. How many consorts have you killed—and eaten?"

"They all went willingly." It pauses, then admits. "Well, willingly enough."

"I'm surprised you didn't take care of these two yourself," the man says, nodding at the corpses of the two men lying on the barren stone.

"I wanted to see you do it. It's been such a long time since I've witnessed your treachery." One of the insect's mid-legs shifts. Loose bones skitter away across the hard ground. There are quite a few of them, the man now notices. "Besides, I dined already."

"I was wondering why there wasn't more of a reception committee."

"I was hungry. Humans always were my favorite, especially the grubs. So succulent." It finishes its grooming and stands. Balanced on its rear two sets of legs, its head is nearly twelve feet off the ground.

"You don't belong in this place any more than the paladin," the man says.

"He was a fool."

"Yes, well, that's a paladin for you. No sense of humor."

"Watching you, on the other hand, was most entertaining. You are astonishingly amoral, even for a human." The mantis takes a delicate step forward, raising the oversized, serrated claws. The human has seen one of its kind snatch up a full-grown oxen with such claws. He takes a step back.

"Weren't you afraid one of them would kill me and spoil your fun?"

"Not at all," the mantis says, taking another step forward. Its huge, opaque eyes appear almost sightless to a human, but they lock onto the man unerringly. "You excel at slaughter. I particularly enjoyed watching you kill your own child."

It takes another step forward.

The man takes two steps back, edging to one side, his eyes never leaving the giant insect. "He was really more his mother's son."

"Him, I was tempted to eat—if only to see the look on your face."

"I imagine the look on his face would have been pretty comical as well. To come all this way for nothing. You might take his example to heart. Think of it as a parable."

"What lesson could you hope to teach me? Humans are no more than talking meat."

"Harsh. And untrue. As I recall, I taught you a great deal."

"I remember everything. You betrayed my people, sold millions into living death, plundered our breeding grounds to provide generation upon generation of mindless slaves..."

"Would it make a difference if I said I was sorry?"

The insect slides forward in a rush, seizing claws at the ready. "Your pain will be a thing beyond measure," it hisses in its dry voice.

The man backs away almost as fast as the other approaches, keeping the point of his blade high. The strength of the insect's claws is immense, and their speed—

It strikes. The man has only an instant's warning. There is a sliding ring of steel, and then the man is out of range, his wrist aching with the force of the parry.

The insect follows. "You will suffer for an eternity," it whispers. "I will peel the skin from your body. I will crush your bones until you are a shapeless slug. I will feast upon your flesh until I have carved you into an exquisite work of horror and parade you through the streets of Hell. One day, when I weary of your agony, I may even let you beg for death."

The man circles to the left, trying to stay out of the range of both claws at once. "So, an apology is out of the question?"

The insect moves forward even faster. The man continues his retreat, splitting his attention between the menace before him and the ground at his back. If he stumbles, it will be over in an instant.

Or rather, it will have just begun.

He risks a glance behind him. Quickly, but not quickly enough. The insect has been waiting for this moment. It strikes with both claws.

The man leaps back, trying to counter in the same instant. One claw wrenches the sword from his hand. The other strikes him in the chest. The blow knocks him head over heels. He feels the claw slide across his armor without finding purchase.

He rolls to his feet, the insect looming above him, and watches as it crumples the sword in its claw as if the blade were made of tin. The mantis raises its other claw to strike again—

And the man lifts the sword named *Remorse*. It blazes like a star in his hand.

The mantis hesitates, startled.

They strike in the same instant.

A serrated claw falls to the ground. The insect rears back, staring at its severed appendage.

And the man is moving. Forward, beneath the body of the

mantis.

The insect backs away, turning in an attempt to keep the other in sight. The man changes direction as it does so, slipping between the legs on the other side. Then he is on its back, climbing the rigid shell.

It feels for him with its remaining claw. The man shears it off at the second joint and keeps climbing.

Reaching the insect's upper thorax, the man drives the point of the blade into the thick column of chitin just behind the head. It used to take a hammer and spike to do this, he recalls, but the shining blade digs into the hard material as if it were softened clay.

The mantis spins frantically, trying to throw the man off. "You cannot do this! You are a *thing!*" it shrieks, its scream like a maddened calliope.

The point of the blade finds the nerve junction hidden beneath the shell and severs it. As it does so, the screeching voice falters, then falls silent. The mantis jerks and stumbles, slowing by turns until it comes to a shuddering stop.

Stillness.

The man maintains his position on its back for a moment longer, regaining his breath. When the giant insect makes no further movements, the man works the sword free and settles himself on the narrow shoulders, one leg to either side of the armored neck.

"I did warn you," he murmurs. "Parables can be a bitch."

The insect makes no reply. The man does not expect one.

Holding the sword in one hand, the man reaches for the sensitive antennae with the other. Beneath him, the insect turns obediently in response to his touch, toward the lights of the city where they climb into the dark and empty sky.

The man cannot be certain, but he thinks he's going to like it here. He considers the blade in his hand. "I think I'll name you *Remorseless*," he says, then looks at his old enemy. "Unless you think that's too on the nose?"

The giant insect says nothing. The man clucks his tongue and gives the antennae a quick twitch. "Let's go, old girl."

Together they set off down the road, leaving the Gates of Hell behind.

A Warning Agaynste Woldes

By Zachary Bos

Ech night and through ech night the forest

a chirche is, from the final note of maghrib to

the waking call of fajr. What chapelgoers then

are there embowered? Not such as we.

Them, enough to know, whose rites are not

ours, nor calendar or communion...

We are to them profane who wander murklins

Uncreeded and unavysèd, we who do not

set root and stay fixèd there to murmur season

to season in worship. Worship of which

divinities, then which lord, which lade? Majnun,

ask not. When you hear the rattle of white

wooden charms hanging from the branches of

the knuckle-oak, hurry thou home. Such trespass

irremissible is; mercy a grace of the warm and

quyke only is. Hwaet; let me teach you...

The barkbound rune, a hierogram: sacred sign.

The ritual in the deerne grove, hierolatry is:

worship of sacred things. The monelicht which

silver-white stains the muscheron below, stains

the misteltan ahigh, hierurgy is: a sacred dance,

dreamed by congregants bewildered by

grove-spirits. Their dreams moss-drapèd are

that call down certain hungers from the stars—

and bodies have they none, bread or blood.

The air in the soughing branches, a malison is.

Forthy, enter not their chirche at night.

The Skulls of Ghosts

By Charles Gramlich

On the walls of dread Sar'thuum,

the carrion birds croaked a name.

Everyone heard it,

the living and the dying,

from palaces, to filthy hovels,

to the warrens where the rats danced.

The name was Krieg.

I: The Plague Gate

Krieg came to the Gate of Devils, in the wall of a city known as Sar'thuum. There were no guards. No one wanted to enter the city in these bleak days, though many were leaving. Most of the city's wealthy had already escaped.

Krieg shouldered through the fleeing throng. Among the crowded poor, he saw those who carried the ghost-marks—pale, skull-shaped discolorations that indicated the first stage of plague.

If left unchecked, the disease would soon spread through the countryside, Krieg knew, and to other cities, perhaps to other lands. It did not concern him.

For a moment, a squat, muscled warrior of the pesh-ka-li stood in front of Krieg, but he stepped aside after meeting the big warrior's cold eyes. The pesh-ka-li were mercenaries and gladiators. They worshipped death; they recognized its many forms. This one, it appeared, was not yet prepared to sacrifice himself to his god.

Once inside the gate, Krieg turned from the main thoroughfare toward a riverfront area known as The Sink. The clamor of frightened people fell behind. He passed merchant booths with no one left to service them. Foodstuffs were gone, and any weapons. But some forgotten goods still remained on display, with no takers. The streets were lorn and empty.

Krieg reached a barricade. Blood splashed the cobblestones. Bodies lay about. Black flies buzzed; maggot moths fluttered. The fight had been recent, for the stink was of fresh blood instead of rot. Someone had made a stand here, but the barricade had been breached. The black-eyed warrior passed through and continued on his way. In the refuse around him now, small fires flickered.

As he neared The Sink, three men in hoods and black cloaks charged at Krieg. Perhaps they wanted his armor and weapons. He did not draw his axe. The three had not timed their attacks well. One reached Krieg seconds before the others. Ducking beneath a swinging cudgel, Krieg's hands caught a belt and a neck. He lifted his assailant effortlessly, slammed him down again across a knee.

While the man screamed with the agony of a broken back, Krieg shoved his ruined body into the path of his fellows. One stumbled. As Krieg straightened from his crouch, he grasped the second foe's head and snapped his neck with a savage twist.

The last foe was a fool. He did not break off his attack but lunged in with short sword flashing. Krieg slipped to one side, caught the swordsman's hand and twisted. A raw shriek burst from the man's lips; bones ground audibly together as his blade was turned inevitably upward to point at his own face.

The assailant's hood fell back, revealing swarthy skin marked by plague skulls. A topknot of greasy reddish hair invited a hold. Krieg grabbed it, slammed the man's face forward onto the sword. Once, twice, thrice. Wiping his hand on the man's cloak, the black-eyed warrior let the body fall like a burden he'd grown tired of.

Though carrion birds followed him with hope after that, no one else troubled him.

II: The Waterfront

Sar'thuum's walls rose along the banks of the River Lhan. Threads of black smoke rolled across the waterfront. Any ships that could float had long since been commandeered for an escape. Krieg saw a family gathering wood to make a raft. The father hefted a chunk of firewood as a threat but the scarred warrior passed him by with scarcely a glance.

An inn loomed out of the growing smoke. Its sign read: AMMA'S PLACE. Krieg recalled why he'd come here. In a village far to the north named Vehnda, at a common well where he'd stopped for a drink, he'd met a girl-child of no more than six. While the warrior stood with a water bucket to his lips, a cold wind had brushed him, chilling his sweat. The child grunted. Her eyes rolled fish-belly white back in her head. She spoke a single word in a voice that could not be hers: "Amma!"

And so, Krieg had come to Sar'thuum, to this place.

The inn was boarded up from the inside. Krieg ripped the door back, then pressed his huge hands against the interior planks and began to exert his strength. Muscles corded along his shoulders and down his arms. The wood bowed, giving way in a shriek of nails. Krieg ducked through the opening into the inn. The shadows stank of stale beer and musk.

"Don't move!" a female voice commanded.

A young woman with a crossbow stood at the top of a set of stairs, her face marred with translucent plague skulls. The weapon shook in her hands.

"I seek Amma," Krieg said.

"For what reason?"

"My own."

The woman stiffened. "Tell me who you are or I'll shoot!"

Krieg looked beyond the woman. A door stood open to a room just behind her.

"Amma!" Krieg called. "Do you live?"

The woman gasped but did not fire. She gasped again when a quavering voice replied to Krieg's question.

"Krieg! Is that you? Go away! The plague. Inga and I both have it."

Krieg started toward the stairs. The young woman, Inga no doubt, threatened again with her crossbow. "I swear I'll shoot!"

"Not with that ancient piece," Krieg said. "The bowstring is rotted."

Stalking past Inga, Krieg entered the room at the top of the stairs. The windows were open for light and air, but wisps of smoke had also begun to creep in. An old woman—Amma—lay on sweat-soaked sheets. Her eyes were fever-gold. The plague skulls on her face had multiplied and darkened, turning her skin purple—the last stage of the disease.

"Krieg," Amma said. "You shouldn't have come."

"I received a message."

Amma looked confused. "But how? I sent no message."

"Sorcery called me to Sar'thuum," Krieg replied. "It used your name."

Amma was a big woman. She seemed to shrink now inside her thin gown. But her voice was clear as she burned the last of her strength. "Not the Ten!" she said. "Surely not the Ten!"

"Not a member of the Ten," Krieg said. "I would have known. But it had the stink of that sorcerer's circle. Someone linked to them."

The woman named Inga spat a name, "Kolthus!"

Krieg waited.

"A year ago," Amma said. "Our king brought a wizard named Kolthus to serve in his palace. Though it was soon rumored the king served Kolthus instead."

"He caused the plague," Inga said.

Again, Krieg waited.

"The first cases appeared here in the Sink, the poor quarter," Amma explained. "But many believe it was experiments by Kolthus that set the evil in motion."

"And you?" Krieg asked.

"I have not seen the man's face," Amma said. "He wears a mask of purple silk. But the aura he bears suggests he is capable of such, and more."

"As bad as the Ten?"

Amma shook her head, then winced at the pain the movement caused her. Krieg's fists tightened. Inga moved to the older woman's bedside, took her hand.

"None are as bad as the Ten," Amma said after a moment. "But you know that. After the time we spent as 'guests' in their nightmare dungeon."

"Their payment comes," Krieg said.

Amma nodded slowly. "You saved me there. You saved others. But in return...."

"I can't save you now," Krieg said.

Inga winced at the warrior's words. Amma smiled. "Honest to the last," the older woman said. "My plague marks must be as purple as a rich man's robe by now. Even though Inga," she smiled at her younger companion, "insists they are not and will give me no mirror to look for myself." Amma glanced back at Krieg. "I wish you hadn't come. But I'm glad to see you one last time."

Krieg nodded, stepped closer and reached down to grasp Amma's limp hand. She tried to squeeze his fingers; he barely felt the pressure. After a moment, he stepped back.

"Sleep well, Amma."

Inga followed Krieg as he left the room. She spoke to him on the stairs, in a whisper so Amma would not hear.

"You could stay. Give her comfort. Have you no feelings?"

Krieg did not pause or look back. "When she's gone, leave. The city will burn."

III: The Palace

Krieg's route to the palace was marked by signs of savage fighting: hacked bodies, spent weapons, blood. Barricades made from overturned wagons had been thrown up and torn down again. Stray dogs prowled among the vultures and carrion crows. But human eyes also watched him. He cared not.

The palace alone showed signs of life. Its iron-barred gate was shut. Men—pesh-ka-li warriors—stood behind it. They drew weapons as Krieg approached. None of them bore any signs of sickness. One warrior wore a crimson cloak marking him an officer.

"Be gone!" that one commanded.

"Is your king already dead?" Krieg asked.

"That's no concern of yours."

Krieg nodded and replied, "So, he is. And now you serve his wizard."

"We serve death. In whatever form it bears."

Krieg's lips curled. "I'll see death then. Or Kolthus, if you prefer."

"Lord Kolthus sees no one. He is dealing with the plague."

Krieg smiled faintly. "Curing it, or causing it?"

"I should kill you for that."

"Later. Send someone to your master. Tell him Krieg is here."

Krieg's confidence gave the guards pause. After a moment, the officer nodded toward a man who hurried into the palace.

"You'll have to give up your axe and daggers," the officer said.

"No."

Several of the pesh-ka-li muttered angrily at Krieg's words. He gave no sign that he noticed.

"You have no power here," the officer insisted. "Turn over your weapons."

"Wait."

The guard returned from the palace with word: "Lord Kolthus says to bring him through but watch him well."

The officer shook his head but unlocked the gate. Other men pulled it back. Krieg passed among them without concern and strode up the marble steps into the palace. Warriors surrounded him with hungry blades. The pesh-ka-li do not believe in killing at a distance. They carried only swords, but there were twelve of them.

A wide front entranceway paneled in marble and lapis lazuli led directly into the throne room. The high seat itself was carved from one piece of quarried obsidian. A man sat there, his head covered in purple cloth without any eyeholes. He wore the garb of a warrior but his arms were thin, his muscles wasted.

Despite the mask, Krieg knew him. "Flavius!"

"You call him Lord Kolthus!" the guard officer snapped.

Krieg paid the guard no mind. He watched the man on the throne, who now struggled slowly to his feet and withdrew the hood hiding his features. Hair of wispy white crowned the man's head; his eyes were filmed with pearl-white cataracts that did not keep him from seeing.

"Krieg!" Kolthus/Flavius said, smiling. "At last."

The Flavius that Krieg had known in the dungeons of The Ten had been a young man, well-muscled and strong. A decade should not have turned *that* man into this wasted scarecrow.

"The years have not been kind, I see," Krieg said.

"Power requires payment," Flavius replied. "More and more all the time."

"The Ten certainly do. But you knew that when you betrayed your fellow prisoners to them."

Flavius—or Kolthus now—shrugged. "Better than dying."

"Yet, others of us lived without doing so."

Kolthus snorted a laugh. "Others? You! Amma! A handful more. Most of them gone now. But..." he shrugged again, "in the end I, too, escaped."

"Fled for your life more likely. When The Ten found you no longer of use."

Kolthus shrugged as he began to walk slowly toward Krieg with his hand out. "All is past now. I grow old. I would make amends for what I did in impetuous youth."

"I doubt it."

"If you will not forgive me for my sake, then for Amma's. I know she still lives but is deathly sick with the plague. I can cure her. You'll notice that none of my soldiers here bear the plague skulls."

Krieg frowned. He did not believe Kolthus wanted to make amends but he probably *could* cure Amma. Two of the sorcerer's guards inching closer distracted his thoughts. Without revealing any tension in his body or face, he readied himself. The guards lunged at him simultaneously. He leaped back.

Grabbing the men's shoulders and using their momentum against them, he slammed the two together. They crashed to the floor. Krieg reached for his double-bitted axe. But Kolthus had thrown himself forward in that same instant, faster than any old man had a right to be. His hand clutched like a talon on Krieg's left wrist.

Everything changed.

IV: The Cemetery

Krieg found himself standing alone in a graveyard, naked and unarmed. A fetid wind did not cool his sweat. A night sky arched overhead, moonless and starless but giving off a sapphire glow bright enough to reveal the world. It wasn't the world he'd inhabited moments before. But it was not unfamiliar.

Before him stretched a field sown with the dead, the graves jumbled like some ruined mandala. Most were unmarked. A few bore headstones with crude titles incised on the rough-hewn granite. By the light of luminescent fungi, he could read them: "soldier, coward, jailer, slave, daughter, son."

The soft, rufous loam of the field had birthed indigo orchids and ruby-heart lilies. Wild briars drooping with pale, thumb-thick berries entangled it all. The scent was not of fruit and flowers, though, but of rotting flesh and ground bone. And the rustle of leaves and petals moving in the breeze sounded like scorpions skittering in the dark.

Krieg spat and watched the earth drink it like nectar. He shook his head. Only a narrow and twisting trail promised a route through the chaos. The black-eyed warrior did not take that path yet. Time would force him to it. But the battle that he knew awaited him at trail's end would wait a little longer, until he had girded himself for war.

Turning, Krieg looked behind him. A hill rose there, covered in a petrified forest. Every crooked trunk, every twisted limb, every dead leaf lay preserved in obsidian perfection. More graves dotted the landscape between the trees. All were marked with stones that bore true names upon them. His mind repeated them, but he did not let his lips move. It would not do well to conjure anything in this place.

Making his way between the trees and graves, Krieg climbed the hill. The burial sites became increasingly elaborate as he continued. Polished granite tombstones gave way to marble crypts veined with threads of argent and gold. The headstones themselves grew in complexity, morphed into basilisks and banshees and beasts with bird wings and human faces.

Then the trees fell away at the apex of the hill. A square block of quartz the size of a house had been laid there, and hollowed to make a sepulcher. A massive bronze horse pawed at the sky from atop the tomb. It glowed as if with moonlight. But there was no moon here.

Krieg muttered the name on the crypt, "Thal." No danger of conjuring *this* soul.

There was no door on the crypt, no lid on the sarcophagus, no body in the tomb. A wool gambeson and accompanying armor lay inside on the floor. The steel gauntlets gripped a sheathed broadsword.

Krieg dressed himself in the armor, then drew the blade. It was straight, double-edged, of grayed steel. The quillons curved forward from the hilt, each tipped with a small metal cup in which a jewel might once have been displayed, although none nestled there now. The sword was not as heavy as the axe he normally carried, but he could adjust. He'd used such weapons enough in the past.

A sound arose from the world outside the crypt, a sound of bones chiming and flesh whispering. Knowing what he would see, Krieg turned and stepped into the open with the sword ready for use.

V: And By Your Deeds They Shall Know You

The black-eyed Krieg took a slow breath. *He* might not have wanted to conjure anything in this desolate place, but someone had. Dark figures stood like scarecrows among the graves. Dozens of them. Men and women. Some were rotted, some fresh. One recent corpse's head hung askew on a broken neck. Another had sword wounds in his face. They all stood swaying, with fingers pointed accusingly at Krieg.

"Killed you all once," Krieg said. "Easy enough to do it again."

A rolling snarl swept the crowd. Those at the front launched themselves toward him. Those behind, less complete, came stumbling. Normally against such numbers, Krieg would place his back to a wall and wait for the enemy to come to him. But he was angry.

With a growl of his own, Krieg leaped forward, his sword swinging, reaping. Limbs and heads flew left and right. At each blow, another figure went down and instantly disintegrated into a pile of thorns and black petals.

Clawed fingers raked at Krieg, drawing bloody streaks down his arms. Such wounds couldn't stop him. And soon only one figure remained before him. Even Krieg paused then. The figure was a child, a blonde girl of seven or eight years. He did not remember her, and it troubled him.

Krieg moved to step around the girl, but she hissed, her mouth drawn impossibly wide over jagged teeth. She hurled herself toward him, mouth snapping, fingers slashing. Krieg waited until the last possible second, then snapped the sword out, stabbing the tip through the girl's neck below the pretty face. The child choked. Black petals and thorns began to spray forth from a wide wound. The child's body collapsed and disintegrated.

Krieg stood for a moment looking down. He sheathed his sword, which was unmarked with gore, and strode on.

VI: In Memory of the Ten

A decade ago, Krieg had spent time in this land. It had not been so bleak then. There were graves, but they were fewer, and better tended. The sky was blue instead of black; the flowers smelled like flowers instead of flesh, and their colors were not all ebony and crimson and pale. Then came The Ten.

In those days, Krieg had borne a true name, one he no longer used. He'd been a wanderer, certainly. A warrior and sometimes a mercenary. But not a killer. Not until The Ten.

All things had changed when he'd come to a small vineyard lying at the foot of a southern mountain. In a place of rich soil and plentiful rain, a place where a woman and her two children lived and worked, he'd found a family. For a time. Before The Ten.

VII: The River

Bearing arms and armor now, Krieg returned to the place where he'd arrived in this barren world. As he'd noted before, a narrow, twisting trail marked the only route through the chaotic landscape of broken stones and dead trees. He strode along it, ignoring the strange whispers scuttling from the petrified forest lying to either side.

Though plenty of shadows flitted through the forest to make the sounds he heard, only once did Krieg see a recognizable figure—a woman in a black shroud. It was Amma, and so he knew she'd succumbed to the plague. She stared at him from beneath a lace mask, accusingly it seemed. He ignored her.

Eventually, he came to a river, one that he knew as The River of Sins Streaming. The flow was a thick, reddish brown, and filled with debris. Rib cages and skulls churned slowly along with the current; some were human, some not. Manacles and chains that should not have floated bobbed on the surface. So too did broken weapons, snapped arrows, splintered lances, and rusted shields. He saw burned books and burned wagons, gossamer gowns torn and slashed, and rotted leather.

Then he gazed across to the other side. The last time he'd been to this land, the river marked its end, with nothing beyond but gray void. But now, a hellscape revealed itself in the same sapphire glow that lit his way. A jagged field of black volcanic rock stretched to the horizon. And lodged atop the lava field rested a ship, a sailing craft with a splintered mast and tattered sail. A dark wound just beneath the bow offered ingress. Krieg took a deep breath.

In this place, the black-eyed warrior had power he did not possess in the everyday world. He turned his stare upon the river; concentration furrowed his brow. The flow of water to his right slowed. Eddies began to roil back upon themselves; detritus churned and screeched as it piled up.

To his left, the current sped. And so, a narrow lane of dry land began to open at the river's center, a passage to the other bank. He stepped down into that passage and strode across, his boots spurning rocks that covered the muddy ground.

As he climbed up the far bank, weakness struck him. His legs threatened to buckle and he stabbed the tip of his sword into the ground for support. Swaying, he glanced back the way he'd come. The opening in the river closed with a clash of waves and rattling flotsam, and he did not think he had the strength to open it again. His way now was forward, only forward. To the end.

VIII: The Ship

Weakness and dizziness plagued Krieg as he made his way across the rough lava field toward the ship. He understood why. On the other side of the river, he'd been moving through the landscape of his own mind; now he found himself in another mind. It was disorienting and unpleasant. And it was the mind of an enemy who wanted him drained and dead.

He reached the ship with numerous cuts on his legs from the stabbing fingers of the lava; he left his blood on the black rocks. But now the wide hole beneath the ship's bow beckoned. And threatened. He stepped inside, into the cargo hold. Only a faint light rose ahead of him, but ever since his time in the dungeons of The Ten, his night vision had been exquisite.

He made his way through jumbled chests and bales of unknown goods. Dust had gathered thickly on everything and hung in the air, making him cough. He reached the wooden stairs leading up from the hold to the deck and paused. A figure sat on the lowest step, a child of no more than six.

"Boy!" Krieg said.

The lad looked up but made no other response. He had no eyes, only torn slits of paper-thin flesh where they should be. Krieg frowned, then moved to step around the lad. With a sudden snarl, the youth opened his mouth wide, showing rows of nail-like teeth.

He lunged for Krieg's leg and the big warrior cuffed him alongside the head to knock him away.

As the boy-creature landed on the floor, he hissed like a rat, then scuttled off into the shadows. He seemed to have grown a tail. Krieg continued up the stairs. The hatch leading onto the deck stood wide, but between him and the open air waited two dire wolves. Emaciated, with fur missing in places, their mouths drooled bloody froth from the ivory teeth bulging their jaws.

"I am not your enemy," Krieg said, "nor your prey." He pushed his black-eyed gaze against the beady rubies that filled the eye-sockets of the wolves. Turning slightly, he pointed below. "That prey lies there."

The wolves snarled. Krieg stepped to one side, against the wall. One after another then, the starving beasts slunk past him and down into the hold. Krieg heard the rat-boy from below give a bleat of terror, then he stepped out onto the deck and slammed the wooden hatch behind him.

The sky was lighter here, like a late evening. The planks he stood on were warped and wet with greenish slime. S-shaped trails marked the slime, but he could see no creatures who might have made them. The only living thing he saw was a man standing bound to the stump of the main mast. Flavius.

He studied the fellow for a moment. Flavius seemed...insubstantial, as if he were no more than a thick mist formed into the shape of a man. His mouth writhed and undulated as he raved quietly to himself in words Krieg could not make out. His thin limbs jerked beneath the silver ribbons binding them.

As Krieg stepped closer, he found that Flavius was truly skin and bones. The big warrior could see through the man's parchment thin dermis to the skeleton beneath, with no flesh or organs to block his view. Flavius should not have been capable of any semblance of life. And yet, he suffered like the living.

Krieg looked away. "Kolthus!" he called. "I'm here."

A chain rattled. A piece of fallen sail, once white but now the color of aged ivory and stained with the rust patches of old blood, winched itself into the air. Beneath it rested a chair made from the linked forms of living rats. In the chair sat Krieg.

IX: Krieg à Deux

"At last!" Kolthus/Krieg said. "I was growing tired of waiting."

"Unlikely," Krieg replied. "Since there is no time truly in this place."

"So, you know where you are?"

"Still in the palace of Sar'thuum. Though it does not appear as such."

Kolthus/Krieg shook his head. "This ship and its world are no illusions. I forced you into *your* mind, and finally into my own. Here I am strong and you are weak. Here you will die. And your form will be forfeit for my purposes."

"Even your time serving The Ten could teach you nothing. How is it they did not kill you?"

Kolthus/Krieg laughed. "Oh, they tried. Their curse is the primary reason why I've aged so rapidly. But I anticipated their actions and stored up enough of their gold and magic to flee before they finished their game. I'm sure they were surprised to find me gone."

"I'm sure they hope to rectify that mistake."

A wry chuckle sounded. "Of course. But once I have your body and skills, I will have a chance to fight them. You're the only man they ever feared. And the only one to escape them. Before now."

"I don't think I'm going to let you have my body."

"You have no choice."

Krieg studied...himself. In height, well above six feet. In weight, above seventeen stone. Dark hair to the shoulders, tinted with silver. A face carved with scars. Chain mail armor and a black, twin-bladed axe in the thickly callused hands.

Krieg hefted the sword *he* held. His muscles trembled and he could feel the weakness that Kolthus had spoken of working its way through him. He ignored it, stepped forward, then charged.

Kolthus/Krieg reared up from his seat, the black axe flashing. Moving with incredible speed, he blocked Krieg's sword as it swung toward him, then hooked with the haft of the big weapon. The pommel at the tip of the axe's haft slammed into Krieg's shoulder, doing little damage but knocking him sideways.

He twisted the sword in his hand, slashed backward at Kolthus's unarmored legs. Kolthus leaped over the blade, came crashing down to the deck on his feet so the whole ship shuddered.

Krieg spun. A thrust with the sword was hammered aside. Krieg dodged as Kolthus chopped the axe at him. The tip screeched along Krieg's chest plate, cutting a thin line through the steel. Krieg struck back with all his strength. The black axe intervened. For a moment, the two men stood toe to toe, straining. Krieg was thrown backward.

Krieg's heart pounded; sweat slicked him. He was weak as a child, and every second drained his strength further and fed it into Kolthus. He had one chance. He circled his foe. Kolthus turned with him, a smirk of victory on his familiar face. When Krieg reached the mast where the living husk of Flavius was bound, he stopped long enough to cut through the ribbons and free the muttering creature.

"You can't kill it," Kolthus taunted. "It barely even exists anymore in this place."

"I don't intend to kill it," Krieg returned.

He shoved the shambling form toward Kolthus, though it was like pushing smoke. The wizard thrust it aside with a snarl. Flavius keened as if that touch burned. Krieg charged again, using nearly the last of his strength.

Kolthus chopped with the axe. Krieg dodged past him to the right. With dazzling speed and strength, Kolthus/Krieg turned the chop of the axe into a side-to-side slice that glittered with black-shine.

Krieg was there, right in the line of that deadly blow. But he'd hooked his sword arm around the figure of Flavius, and now yanked him into the path of the axe. Flavius flickered in one place, reformed in another. Even as Kolthus shouted, "No," the curved edge of his stolen weapon sheared through the skin and bone structure of his true form—Flavius.

"I'll let you kill it," Krieg said softly.

Flavius fell into two halves; empty skin flapped; bones rattled like dice on the deck. Kolthus/Krieg's face showed shock, and fear. The world of the ship wavered. The palace of Sar'thuum snapped into existence around them, as if less than a second had passed since Kolthus first grabbed his wrist.

Krieg looked down as strength flowed back into him like a flood. The old man that was Kolthus/Flavius still had hold of his left wrist but Krieg's free hand had already grasped his axe. *His* axe. He drew it over his shoulder. The twin blades gleamed. He hacked downward, cutting through Kolthus's arm just below the elbow. The sorcerer screamed as blood geysered.

Kolthus staggered back, eyes wide as wine cups. Krieg struck him again with the axe, crushing his head like a boot stomping an overripe fruit. The sorcerer's pesh-ka-li guards stood with their mouths agape.

"Run!" Krieg said.

They did so.

X: End in Flame

Krieg came out from the palace into the streets. The fires that were already burning in the city began to leap and grow, as if the sorcerer's death fed them. The big warrior started toward the main gate but paused as he saw the woman, Inga, running up to him.

The plague skulls on her face seemed less pronounced, a sure sign that Kolthus had been responsible for that evil as well.

"Amma is dead," Inga panted.

"I know," Krieg replied. "I told you to flee."

"I have nowhere to go."

Krieg grasped her wrist. "For now, you go with me." Pulling her behind him, he ran for the gates of dread Sar'thuum. The dying city began to scream.

The Headsman's Melancholy

By Joseph Andre Thomas

12-9-1399

Today, I met a man I had killed before.

I walked to the Tower Hill at first light, the clouds above a distinctly London slate-grey. Upon my shoulder lay Long-badger, the best Headsman's axe that ever was, of the finest Damascus crucible steel, her blade silver-and-black.

A small crowd of about twenty was gathered. The Tower Guards had erected the Headsman's Block—my "bread-and-butter," if you will—and brought out a clean head-basket (though dark stains betrayed its employ). Present were the cold shapes of the Lord Privy Seal and the London Chancellor. As usual, neither spoke to me. Also present was a red-faced Priest to administer Last Rites.

The Condemned today were three: a Spy for the French rebels; a fat-nosed Usurer; and a Pickpocket whose robbery had turned to murder. I walked behind the Priest as he took their last words, noting each face. I never speak to the Condemned, though I always look them in the eye. I learned to slaughter livestock upon my family farm at Shrimpshir—and I learned to respect the slaughter. Whether it be a murderer or a beef-cow, one must always show respect. So I look them in the eye. .

The Spy cried he was being unfairly lumped with his countrymen. The Usurer made jowled whimpers that he was a misunderstood but legitimate Business-man. The Pickpocket remained silent when the Priest asked his last words.

He was in his middle-twenties, I guessed, with a long tuft of greasy brown hair, thinning at the temples. His eyes were deep green, tinny in the grey morning light. A hint of a smile crossed his lips when he noticed me.

I had several vexing realizations at once: that I had seen this man before, that it had been on this very Hill...and that I had beheaded him.

I tried to hide my amazement as I returned to the Block. It was impossible, of course. I had not *killed* this man before. He must be the twin to a previous Condemned, perhaps a cousin of strong resemblance. As the Priest anointed the foreheads of the three Condemned with Holy Water, I tried to recall the circumstances of the earlier execution. He had been guilty of robbery or skamelar, some such knavery. It had been years ago, however. Likely I misremembered the original man's face.

Though the Usurer was a large man, Long-badger swept through the fat of his neck with ease. The modest crowd clapped politely as his big head fell into the head-basket. The Spy thrashed and wept. His head popped off like a wine cork. The crowd cheered vigorously.

The Guards brought over the Pickpocket. He looked about the Hill, disinterested, as if this were not a particularly serious situation and, if it were not too much trouble, could we please hurry things along?

As I lowered his head onto the Block, he said, softly: "Why hello, Jack. Good to see you again."

I clutched Long-badger's handle in surprise—then swung her with more force than I can ever recall doing so before. There was a splatter like melon smashing, a sickening pop as his spinal cord violently separated. His head missed the head-basket and rolled to the edge of the grass, spattering blood on the nearby spectators. The shocked crowd took a moment before applauding.

A Guard retrieved the man's head. I could swear it retained something of his smile.

13-9-1399

In my haste to record the above entry, I neglected to introduce myself. My name is Jack Marvell, Headsman for the Court of the newly-crowned King Henry IV. My duties are that of any Headsman: to carry out Royal Executions. I do so, I believe, with Grace and a Goodly-manner.

I write this at my small wooden desk in my small wooden home in St. Paul. I am...not well. Something is wrong with my mind, a terrible Melancholia, I am told. My drinking-friend and Poet, Geoff, offered this solution: a diary. A vessel for my thoughts.

"Writing," he said, slurring the words together, "is medication for the Soul."

It has been two months since King Richard II was deposed. Richard appointed me after I distinguished myself at Radcot Bridge and gifted me Long-badger. Richard was a very good King. I previously thought this Bolingbroke—who now titles himself in the line of Henry—a Rake and Usurper, but he has retained me as Headsman and allowed Richard to live out his days at Castle Pontefract. Perhaps he is not so bad. These political machinations are an act of God, and God often confuses me.

Some might assume this Melancholia comes from my line of work, but no—the King's orders are ordained by God, thus I and Long-badger are instruments of God's will. I have nothing to feel guilty about.

23-9-1399

I have all about me Darkness. Shadows, shadows that never recede. A veil in my mind keeps the light out. I can see no value in [*writing illegible*] done about it.

Oh—some of the ink has smudged. I am weeping and will weep until my face becomes sore and I run out of tears, then fall asleep. As most of my nights go. I told Geoff this diary would not help, but [*writing illegible*] try anything.

I think I may be too drunk for diary-writing.

1-10-1399

Has someone been in my home? Rooting about? When I awoke this morning, the door to my wardrobe was ajar and some pieces of clothing on the floor. My writing ledger was displaced, too, some ink spilled. The chair was moved, too. I checked on my coin purse and my axe. Nothing of value appears to be missing.

Next door, I caught my neighbour, a knacker dressing in his ruddy leathers for a long day of removing St. Paul's dead dogs and horses, and asked him if he noticed anyone entering my home last night. He replied that he'd heard me stumble in well past midnight, but that was it. I explained the situation and asked if he'd noticed anyone else. He asked, sneering, how in the Hell would I even be able to remember where everything was, the state I was in last night?

Though bluntly put, he had a point. However, the feeling remains: a gentle but persistent *wrongness* in the air of my home, as if something has disturbed the very aether.

But perhaps the knacker was correct. Perhaps I was simply too drunk. Perhaps I am the stranger in my own home.

15-10-1399

Today, I went to see the Physician of my Parish. He had me spit into a kerchief, then examined the ejaculation with two small metal rods. He *hmm*'d and *yes*'d as he worked.

"Mostly red, but a surplus of black bile, you see?"

It all looked phlegm-coloured to me.

"It is a poor combination. I am unsurprised you feel morose. Have you been praying?"

"Morning and night."

"Drinking plenty of red wine?"

"Oh yes."

"Has anything happened recently," asked the Physician, "to cause your Melancholy?"

"I have always felt this way," I said.

The Physician shook head. "Nonsense—this type of Melancholia is brought on by a simple imbalance of the humors. We'll find the root."

I wish that I had said: *I think the Darkness has been with me always, since Shrimpshir at least, and growing—growing larger and more Soul-devouring with every passing day, with every mundane tragedy of my life, with every head I lop off. I have left countless dead but will myself leave this life having made no impression on anyone living. There is no single cause of my pain. It is life that is killing me.*

Instead I said, "All right."

He took the cuff of my shirt and rolled it back, examining the forearm. "Well, you seem relatively clean. I am not certain why, but you give the impression of being filthy."

I told him about the diary and what the Poet said about giving a voice to the Soul. The Physician turnt his nose as though I had let out a great fart.

"You're writing *Poetry*?"

"No," I said. "No—not Poetry. Prose. A bit like a History, but only about myself and very boring."

"I suppose that's all right, so long as you are very careful not to let it become Poetry." He sneered. "*Then* you will know that your mind has truly gone rotten."

He went to a cabinet full of medications and pulled down a mustard-coloured phial. "This is an *emetic*—or vomitive. Black bile can be caused by poor digestion. This will purge your stomach." Next he showed me a phial of grey sludge. "This is a *laxatif*. Similar mixture, but for your bowels." He made a motion like crossing himself. "Same Philosophy, either end."

The tinctures within smelled brackish—or one smelled so brackish that it overpowered the other, I am not sure. He promised to consider a leeching regimen if these medications proved ineffective.

17-10-1399

Darkness remains all about me, but now I am shitting and vomiting every hour. My home smells like the Fenlands bogs in blazing summer. I think I will see a different Physician.

26-10-1399

I saw him again.

I sat, in my cups, laughing with my Poet friend at the Heady Runnel in Aldersgate. The rowdy crowd was elbow-to-elbow. Geoff seems to live in Public-houses.

We got to speaking about the diary. I told him that it had not helped. If anything, all this silly writing has only forced me to confront the contents of my mind, something I was not at all keen to do.

He laughed, sloshing ale down his shirt. "That is *precisely* the point, Jack! If something comes out through the diary you find unpleasant, that is your Soul crying out to be heard! Listen!"

Before I could respond, a man by the bar caught my eye.

The man. The Pickpocket.

He was very much not beheaded. He had the same mussy brown hair and jade eyes, I was certain, and wore the same cocky smile upon his lips. He noticed me looking and raised his goblet.

I stood, interrupting Geoff and upending the table. I pushed through the crowd, but when I reached the bar, the Pickpocket was gone. I scanned the room. He was nowhere to be seen. Geoff called out to me, angry about his lost beer.

Outside, the street was empty, save for an old Beggar. I flipped him a mark.

"Hoy Mendicant, did you see a man leave the Runnel just now? Muddy brown hair? Striking green eyes? Smug smile?"

The Beggar shook his head and said no, I was the only one to leave in the last half-hour and added, unbidden, that he was extremely perceptive and could be trusted completely. He then bit the mark, which made no sense because it was not Gold.

Geoff was cross with me when I returned, though he had difficulty expressing it in complete sentences. He said I owed him a drink.

I was not so drunk as to be hallucinating. It *was* the same man.

4-11-1399

No—no, no, no. She is gone. My pride and [*writing illegible*] only thing I have upon this Earth that keeps me from ending [*writing illegible*] to find her missing! Gone! Disappeared!

Priceless! I [*writing illegible*] a gift from Good Richard! I have looked everywhere but there is no sign [*writing illegible*] what Monster could do such a thing?

5-11-1399

I did not sleep last night. I was too hysterical. I sat in the corner, viciously sobering, until the first morning light.

When I returned home, the padlock upon my west-facing window had been broken and my furniture overturned. At first, nothing appeared to be missing. Even my coin purse remained untouched. Only when I checked above the wardrobe, Long-badger's home, did I realize what had been taken.

I did not see the ransom note on my desk until this morning: *You and I—Vendris, nocte, The Dog's-Bollocks.*

9-11-1399

The Dog's-Bollocks, a Bishopsgate Ale-house too rank even for me. I arrived just before Midnight and examined the rough crowd, wondering how many of these snaggle-toothed, dirt-smeared faces I would see on the Block one day. The ale tasted yeasty, but I fortified myself none-the-less.

I found him staring at me from a corner table, draped in shadows.

I should have been more shocked by these circumstances, yet all I could feel towards this apparent immortal was red fury.

"Hello," he said, smiling. The noise of The Dog's-Bollocks around us seemed to fade, a bit like quiet rage in the heat of battle. "Thank you for coming."

"Where is Long-badger?" I spat.

"Long...what?" he said, cocking an eyebrow.

"My axe," I said. "Where is it?"

"'Long-badger'," said the Pickpocket. "Where in Hell did that name come from?"

"I do not know. She was named by her Blacksmith."

The man chuckled and waved two fingers at the Barmaid.

"What are you?" I said. "A...a triplet? Angry I killed your brothers? Some imbecile Prestidigitator?"

"Something like that."

"If you are looking for revenge, you are misguided," I said. "I have nothing to do with sentencing. Speak to the Tower Judges or the Lord Privy Seal if you think Justice has been miscarried."

"*Misguided*?" He mocked shock. "You've killed me twice now! I'm not sure revenge has ever been more reasonable."

"I am no murderer. I am an embodiment of the King's Justice."

"Oh no, it's not your fault. Never is, is it? Can't fault a Smithy for the uses of a hammer, can we?" That wormy smile crawled back across his lips. "It's always been easy for you, hasn't it—killing? Ever since Shrimpshir."

I coughed on a mouthful of beer.

"What was the first, Jack? A pig? A lame-legged horse?"

A memory burst through: my home, the family farm. Phoronis, my father's favourite milk-cow, had been gashed by a wolf and the wounds would not heal. *Come*, said my father, vast and serious. He walked me to the barn. *It would be best*, he explained, *if yor first were an animal ye knew. Harden ye up.*

122

Impassive, he shoved a wooden bit into Phoronis' mouth and placed an axe in my hand. He tapped the sad-looking cow's forehead and said: *Aim betwixt the eyes*. I did. Phoronis convulsed viciously. Blood surged from the wound. *How do ye feel?* he asked me afterwards. I told the truth: that I felt nothing. It had really been quite easy. He nodded. *Good.*

"You—how did you—who are you?" I sputtered.

"People make such a stink of it, but it's quite easy to end a life. Might bother the squeamish, but someone's got to do it—no?"

"I have a retinue of Guards by the Bishopsgate."

"No, you don't," he snorted. "Murder is one thing, but lying? *That's* beneath you, Jack." He dropped his voice. "Really, you meet a man you've put to death twice, and you're not a bit curious?"

I said nothing.

"To answer the question I'm sure you'd ask if you were more level-headed: I don't know how or why I'm still alive. I just am." He leaned in conspiratorially. "Have you ever been married, Jack?"

"No."

"Why not? A dashing success like yourself?"

Because I would not wish this life upon my worst enemy, I thought. "Never met the right woman," I said.

"Let me tell you a story," the Pickpocket said. "Years ago—many years now—I discovered my Wife with another man—a Cobbler! Cuckolding I, a Stonemason? Unthinkable! At first, I was angry. I plotted vengeance. But soon the anger abated, replaced by pain—a gnawing at my Soul. So I went up to Scawfell and threw myself off the tallest cliff I could reach. When I hit the rocks, the pain was unimaginable. I expected death, but it never came. Eventually, I opened my eyes and looked down at my mangled *corpus*—and watched as the flesh and bone knit itself back together"

He glinted at me, as if daring an interruption. "Assuming that it was some kind of Purgatorial hallucination, I went back up to the cliff and did it again. Same bloody results!" He ran a finger around his neck, the neck I had severed weeks ago. "And no one else has had better luck since."

I said nothing.

"Things are much better now." He slugged back his drink. "Throwing myself off that cliff turned out to be the best decision I've ever made."

"And what does that have to do with my axe?"

"I find your single-mindedness admirable," said the green-eyed man.

"Next you will tell me how to grow a tiny Mandrake goblin or prescribe a Faerie Dance cure for my haemorrhoids."

His smile remained, yet somehow, the mirth drained away. "It's not your fault, I know," he said. "You're no murderer."

I drained off the rest of my pint, then grabbed his collar and raised a fist, callused hard as a mailed fist, not sparing a glance towards the bar. I judged the Bollocks would not begrudge its clientele the odd brawl.

"Mercy!" he simpered. "Think, Jack. If my story is hogwash and you kill me, you'll never see Long-badger again."

"Oh, I never planned to kill you," I said, pulling him closer. "Only to thoroughly maim."

"I just need a little money, that's all." He unfolded a piece of paper from his breast pocket. A map of Newgate. He pointed at a thin road. "A rookery can be reached through this alley. £10, that's all I need. Place it beneath the third bird-house from the gate within three nights, and I'll return your axe."

I fixed him with a skeptical glare, but snatched the paper. "£10?"

"£10."

I pocketed the map and rose to my feet. "Whatever happened to them?" I asked.

"Who?"

"Your Wife and Cuckolder."

"Oh! They live. Perfectly happy together!" He laughed. "But I certainly found a way to leave an impression upon them."

12-11-1399

Last night, I staggered drunkenly to Newgate. I took £10. I had spent the afternoon at a Smithy in Cripplegate—reputedly one of the best in London—who showed me his axe-heads and handles, each more beautiful than the last. Each one filled me with sickening despair.

£10 is not so much money to a man in my profession, though I could see how it might be a small fortune to a man like him. I did not believe his "immortality" nightsoil-story, but that he was some poor Mountebank pushed to desperation? That I could believe.

Returning home, however, I was struck: I am paid a £5 stipend by the Crown per every execution. A pretty-penny for ugly work.

£10, his ransom—precisely the cost of two executions.

17-11-1399

The events detailed herein occurred three nights ago. I could not put quill to parchment until now. I did not believe—refused to believe. I have not had a steady hand since.

The night after I visited the rookery in Newgate, I awoke to a keening sound. A bird, perhaps? A fox caught in the house?

No...a man.

A nude man in the corner of my home, hunched in the shadows with his rear-end to me. His skin sagged, the sharp ridges of his spine protruding like a Dragon's scales. He shook violently. I pulled myself up in bed. His tittering reminded me of men on the battlefield suffering from battle madness. Indeed, I initially thought that a lunatic had broken into my home.

Until the fog of sleep faded, and I realized the naked man was *laughing*.

He looked over his shoulder. "Oh, good." His green eyes glistened in the moonlight. "You're awake."

I blinked, too stunned to speak. Something extended from his stomach, like an extra limb. Long and thin—a pole?

"Took some time," he said, "to get it in."

He turned and stepped into the moonlight.

An axe-head—a silver-and-black steel axe-head I knew all too well—was lodged *in his stomach*, as though some great Berserker had swung it into the man's guts with all his might.

He worried at the axe-handle, straining the contents beneath his skin. The cracking of ribs echoed through my home.

He grimaced—and grinned.

"Thought it'd be easy to just, you know, hook it under me guts."

I was too stunned to speak. His body jostled. Bones snapped, bowels shifted. Tears poured from his eyes. Clearly in great pain, he continued to smile.

"Had to prop it up on the ground, stand on an apple-crate," he grunted through tears, "and throw myself on it. Not so easy, impaling yourself upon an axe."

Then he took long, awkward, bow-legged steps up onto my bed. I pressed myself against the wall. The Demon stood over me, his face flushed with effort. He sweated profusely; it spattered my face. His hairy manhood flopped inches from my stomach.

He stood there for a moment, monolithic, like some Pagan nightmare creature.

"All that just to make an impression."

Then the axe came free.

Innards spumed from his chest cavity, exploding forth like the breath of some strange dragon. Hot liquid and entrails poured over me. Intestines, stomach, rib-bones, muscles, cecum, what I thought might be a bit of colon, and one of his lungs—all of it hot and alive and wriggling like snakes.

The man screeched laughter as he eviscerated himself. His blood poured down my face, into my mouth. It seeped between my teeth and beneath my tongue.

I screamed.

His smile was no longer cocky, but overjoyed. He reached into his chest cavity and grabbed hold of something, pulled it out. His heart, I realized, still attached by whatever tubes and capillaries govern the viscera. He hung it out above me with one hand, then used Long-badger's blade to slit the tendons and dropped his heart into my crotch.

I tried to scream again, but my body, my mind, was frozen.

Having severed more than my fair share of heads from more than my fair share of bodies, I knew that oftentimes the body could live for some time after death, through what Heavenly Engine I have no clue. I had seen eyes on severed heads roll in their sockets, lips move as if trying to speak.

This was different—very different.

The madman lorded over me wearing an expression of insane happiness. He panted through grinning teeth. Steam rose from his skin, his chest cavity hollowed but for some jutting, broken ribs and inchoate gore. Flaps of skin hung from the sides of his cavernous stomach, like an ancient man's jowls; his cock and man-hair had been painted red.

He stared down at his work, admiring the abominable mess like some unholy Haruspex.

He held up Long-badger—then let her clatter to the floor.

"As promised."

Then I watched, immobile, as he knelt and began to gather up the viscera in his arms. He slid the gore off my chest and dumped it into a leather sack he had propped open at the end of the bed. He repeated the action, pulling flesh and stomach and bits of bone off me and carrying them back to the sack. He giggled all the while.

"I'm sorry we must part each other's company like this—though sorrier still about how we met." He hoisted up his bag of guts and slung it onto his back like some Haymaker from Hell. "Just your shit luck to have had to kill me, Jack. Really. Enjoy your axe!"

He winked, then walked laughing into the street, naked and dripping slimy blood.

Several long minutes passed before I could move. I slunk off my bed and looked down at Long-badger, covered in blood and meat from the disemboweling. I had almost convinced myself the event had been a horrid, vivid nightmare, until I walked to the well and began to wash. Layer upon layer of blood sloughed off my face. It took six buckets of water before I could see skin again.

I noticed my neighbour, the knacker, watching me as I washed, a horrified look upon his face. He appeared as though he might vomit, but when our eyes met, he calmed.

Oh, it is just the nasty Headsman, his relieved expression said. *Perhaps this is not so strange a situation for him.*

31-1-1400

I have been ignoring this diary. I have decided I do not much like writing. All it has made me do is face my thoughts, something I typically avoid. Wine and ale help, briefly, but sobriety always finds me, like a bleary-eyed tax-man, and the black matter of my mind takes charge.

I cannot sleep. Whenever I close my eyes, I see red: a chest ripping open, entrails spilling all over me, drowning, choking. Even the Darkness, red.

In the day, however, it is his words from The Dog's-Bollocks that haunt me, clanging about my brain like the Bells of Westminster: "...the best decision I've ever made."

I think that I would like to stop thinking entirely.

12-2-1400

I have been asked to kill the King.

Not the sitting King—*my* King. Richard.

131

I received an emissary from Bolingbroke—I *spit* his name and refuse to call him Henry—with a missive requesting my presence at Castle Pontefract to-morrow. It was full of vague language expressing Bolingbroke's desire to witness my "talents" and "aid in the noble transition."

"I deeply hope," he wrote, "that you share my vision for a new, peaceful England."

The letter was not specific, but its meaning was clear. There is only one use for a Headsman, and only one prisoner at Pontefract.

I sit here at my desk, considering my choices.

The first: I accede. Go to Pontefract, do the deed, return home, ingratiate myself in Bolingbroke's court, and...what? Continue my vacuous existence? Drink the nights away until called upon to behead the odd Adulterer?

The second: I leave. Escape London entirely, live elsewhere. I have heard that the beaches are endless and it is always sunny in the Mediterranean. However, leaving will be difficult. I am well-known to the Guards. I could never return to England. Breaking a King's Ultimatum would be a death-sentence.

The third: I find a more...permanent solution. One I have been considering for some time. Long-badger's edge is sharp. Just a few quick moments and all my problems would disappear.

Or perhaps, like the Pickpocket, I would find a surprise on the other side. I would be all right with that, I think, living forever. Do anything, go anywhere. Travel to the Orient, walk across the ocean floor to find what is on the other side. I could be anyone. I could walk straight to the future.

Is there magic in those mountains? Perhaps I will take a trip to Scawfell.

Live forever or not at all.

I am tired.

This will be my last entry. To Hell with it. This bloody diary has not helped me at all.

14-2-1400

"Soaring O'erhead"

A heart that cries with wings that beat the sky,

A dreaming bird am I in the skies apart,

Dreaming [*writing illegible*] my eyes,

Amongst the clouds, my eagle-shaped heart,

Bright feathers high, my fledgling wings spread

fast,

[*writing illegible*]

Above grey clouds I'll soar in flight at last,

To dream-land's embrace I'll—

[*remainder of pages torn out*]

About the Authors

Zachary Bos lives in Massachusetts, and studied creative writing in the graduate poetry workshops at Boston University. He runs a small press, Pen & Anvil, and operates Bonfire Bookshop.

Amelia Gorman lives in Eureka where she spends her free time exploring forests & tide pools and fostering dogs. Her fiction appears in *Nightscript 6* and *Cellar Door*. Read her poetry in *Dreams & Nightmares, Penumbric* and *Vastarien*. Her chapbook, the Elgin-winning *Field Guide to Invasive Species of Minnesota*, is available from Interstellar Flight Press. Her microchapbook, *The Worm Sonnets*, is available from The Quarter Press.

Charles Gramlich is a teacher and writer who lives in the piney woods of Louisiana. He blogs at http://charlesgramlich.blogspot.com and is happy to connect on Facebook.

Dave Henrickson has a background in computers, engineering, and oceanography but always wanted to be a writer. Or an artist, maybe a dancer. He currently lives in Virginia and spends his free time writing, reading, and killing monsters with his wife Abbie.

Joe Koch writes literary horror and surrealist trash. Their books include *The Wingspan of Severed Hands, Convulsive,* and *The Couvade,* which received a Shirley Jackson Award nomination in 2019. His short fiction appears in publications such as *Vastarien, Southwest Review, PseudoPod, Children of the New Flesh,* and *The Queer Book of Saints.* Joe is also co-editor of the art horror anthology *Stories of the Eye.* He/They. Find Joe online at horrorsong.blog and on Twitter @horrorsong.

Jonathan Olfert writes Stone Age fantasy and lesser genres. He has made and used a plethora of Paleolithic tools. He and his family live in Atlantic Canada. He is not a mammoth.

Joseph Andre Thomas is a writer and literature teacher living in Vancouver, British Columbia. He is a graduate of the University of Toronto's MA in Creative Writing program. A recipient of the Avie Bennett Emerging Writer scholarship and the Canada Master's scholarship, Joseph's writing has appeared in the anthologies *Howls From Hell* (longlisted for a Bram Stoker Award—'Superior Achievement in an Anthology'), *Howls from* *the Wreckage*, and *Collage Macabre: An Exhibition of Art Horror*, he has work forthcoming in the debut anthology from Black Cat Books and *The Darkness Beyond the Stars: An Anthology of Space Horror*.

K. H. Vaughan is a refugee from academia with a Ph.D. in clinical psychology. He writes dark fiction and poetry and is the director of programming for NecronomiCon Providence. His collection of weird tales, *This Is The Table Where We Wash Our Dead*, will be published in 2024.

Made in the USA
Las Vegas, NV
04 March 2025